APP

VOLUME 3 OF THE 1984 TRILOGY

Apple S

A NOVEL

ÉRIC PLAMONDON

TRANSLATED FROM THE FRENCH BY
DIMITRI NASRALLAH

ESPLANADE
Books

THE FICTION SERIES AT VÉHICULE PRESS

Published with the generous assistance of the Canada Council for
the Arts, the Canada Book Fund of the Department of Canadian
Heritage, and the Société de développement des entreprises cul-
turelles du Québec (SODEC). We acknowledge the financial support
of the Government of Canada through the National Translation
Program for Book Publishing, an initiative of the *Roadmap for
Canada's Official Languages 2013-2018: Education, Immigration,
Communities*, for our translation activities.

Esplanade Books editor : Dimitri Nasrallah
Cover design: David Drummond
Photo of author: Justine Latour/Le Quartanier
Typeset in Minion and Futura by Simon Garamond
Printed by Marquis Printing Inc.

Originally published as *Pomme S* by Le Quartanier, 2013

LIBRARY AND ARCHIVES CANADA CATALOGUING IN PUBLICATION

Title: Apple S : a novel / Éric Plamondon ; translated from the
French by Dimitri Nasrallah.
Other titles: Pomme S. English
Names: Plamondon, Éric, 1969- author. | Nasrallah, Dimitri, 1978-
translator.
Series: Fiction series at Véhicule Press.
Description: Series statement: The fiction series at Véhicule Press
| Volume 3 of the 1984 trilogy
Identifiers: Canadiana (print) 20190225378 | Canadiana (ebook)
20190225386 | ISBN 9781550655421
(softcover) | ISBN 9781550655483 (HTML)
Classification: LCC PS8631.L32 P6413 2020 | DDC C843/.6—dc23

Distribution in Canada by LitDistCo;
in the U.S. by Independent Publishers Group, Chicago

Published by Véhicule Press, Montréal, Québec, Canada
vehiculepress.com

Printed in Canada.

...in my weariness, I realized that my life had to have some meaning all the same, and would have one if only certain events, defined as desirable, were to occur.

—GEORGES BATAILLE

Thus expressing a human need, I have always wanted to write a book ending with the word 'mayonnaise'.

—RICHARD BRAUTIGAN

CONTENTS

1

OPENING

Once upon a time in America there was an adopted child who became a billionaire.

2

WITHOUT A SILVER SPOON

Gabriel Rivages is born in Quebec City in 1969. He grew up with the adage, "When you're born without a silver spoon, you're born without a silver spoon." If he'd been raised in the United States, he would have been told, "If you really want something, you can make your dream come true." At forty years old, Gabriel Rivages realizes that, all his life, he's fought against a saying. When you're born without a silver spoon...

3

ARBEIT MACHT FREI

Gabriel Rivages discovers literature because of surrealism. At twenty-three years old, he stumbles across André Breton's *Manifesto*. That introduces him to Comte de Lautréamont. Diving into *Les Chants de Maldoror*, Rivages had never encountered a text so powerful, so physical. The book by Lautréamont, whose real name was Isidore Ducasse, is at once a carnal and intellectual adventure. You can't walk away from it unscathed. You understand the force that words can have. It's something like the scene with the razor in the eye at the beginning of *Un Chien Andalou*. It's a boxing round with no gloves, a wrestling match with no faking, a street brawl with no end.

Lautréamont writes, "I accepted life as an injury, and I defended suicide as a cure to its scars." Rivages can't ask for more. The words sum up exactly what he thinks, along with the famous metaphor of the young man "beautiful like the fortuitous encounter of a sewing machine and an umbrella on a dissection table". That sewing machine is no doubt a Singer, if not a Remington. The *Surrealist Manifesto* is published for the first time in 1924. At the summer Olympic Games in Paris, Johnny Weissmuller

wins the gold medal in the 100-metre free swim, coming
in ahead of Duke Kahanamoku. Four years later, in Nadja,
André Breton writes, "Nothing is to be gained from being
alive, if we have to work."

4

COPYWRITER

In Blade Runner, the replicants are machines that have become as intelligent as humans. They are robots that imitate man to perfection. You can only tell them apart from their pupils. When the leader of the replicants presses his thumbs into the eyes of his creator, you can't help but think of Buñuel's scene with the sliced eyeball. But here we're in Ridley Scott's vision. The story does not belong to Dali, but to Philip K. Dick. We ask questions about humanity. What differentiates us from a machine? Harrison Ford has the leading role. Between Raiders of the Lost Ark and Return of the Jedi, he's at the peak of his glory days.

Before making movies, Ridley Scott produced commercials. When in 1983, the Chiat/Day agency proposed he develop a big-budget ad for a computer company, it suited him very well. The creators thought of him because they wanted a feel along the lines of *Blade Runner,* which had come out the year before. In less than a minute, viewers had to understand that they were in the world of George Orwell's 1984. They want to adapt Big Brother to the flavors of the day. The first film adapted from the novel dates back to 1956.

Today, Apple's 1984 is considered one of the greatest commercials ever made. It is to commercials what Mona Lisa is to the history of painting. It's the crowning achievement of a format. It's Cellini's *Perseus* for televisual propaganda. It swept into the larger culture and sits next to the *Goldberg Variations*, alongside *Citizen Kane*, *Swan Lake*, Tarzan, Don Quixote, and *Joan of Arc*. Thanks to three guys at a Californian ad agency, Macintosh computers become a crucial landmark in the history of personal computing and Steve Jobs emerges as a savior of humanity.

In *Blade Runner*, the machine loses the game. With 1984, Chiat/Day win the Grand Prize at the 31st International Advertising Festival in Cannes. Nobody remembers the anonymous writer who came up with the catchphrase upon which the whole project is based.

The final slogan of the ad ought to be credited to a certain Gary Gussick, copywriter by profession.

Without text, an idea is nothing.

5

MCMLXXXIV

Shot 1 (00:00 – 00:03)
Fade in from black. Exterior tunnel. Zoom in on a cylindrical footbridge encased in glass. An enormous number 14 indicating the floor, the hall, the building? Blue and grey tones create a penitentiary ambiance. A faint rumble and the modulations of a siren blend in with an off-screen voice that says:

Today we celebrate the first

Shot 2 (00:03 – 00:06)
Cross fade. Interior tunnel. A column of grey men marching on foot. The sound of boots is superimposed on the siren and the off-screen voice that continues:

glorious anniversary of
Information Purification

Shot 3 (00:06 – 00:07)
American shot. A blonde female in white bathing suit and red shorts runs toward us in slow motion. She holds a large hammer, a heavy sledgehammer, with two hands.

Directives.

Shot 4 (00:07 – 00:10)
Interior tunnel. Wide shot on the faces of the grey men, who continue their military march, as if hypnotized. Some wear masks. They have shaved heads.

We have created, for the first time

Shot 5 (00:10 – 00:11)
American shot. An anti-riot brigade, all in black, heads covered with helmets and visors, carrying Billy clubs, run toward the camera, toward us, behind the blonde woman (same slow-motion effect as Shot 3).

in all of history,

Shot 6 (00:11 – 00:14)
Interior tunnel. Low-angle shot on the grey men marching. We do not see their faces.

a garden of pure ideology,

Shot 7 (00:14 – 00:16)
Interior tunnel. Close-up shot on the feet of the grey men, who advance inexorably.

where each

Shot 8 (00:16 – 00:16)
The blonde woman continues her run. She appears to get closer.

worker

Shot 9 (00:16 – 00:20)
Interior dark room. A crowd of spectators gathers before

a man in close-up on a giant screen. We discover that he's the one whose voice we've been hearing since the beginning in the off-screen voiceover. We understand that it's toward this room that the grey men are marching. They disperse to the left and right in two rows from a center aisle.

may bloom, secure from the pests of any contradictory

Shot 10 (00:20 – 00:22)
The blonde woman, in close up, continues to approach. She's wearing white socks and red shoes. The brigade of assailants emerges behind her. Her body rises in slow motion. Her breasts sway gently within her white T-shirt.
true thoughts.

Shot 11 (00:22 – 00:25)
Pan shot across the grey men in front of the screen, sitting in rows, with distressed expressions. The scene is bathed in a light that portends the end of the world.
The Unification of Thoughts
is more powerful a weapon

Shot 12 (00:25 – 00:26)
Low-angle shot. Subjective view of motionless spectators, who watch and listen to the man in close up on the screen.
than any fleet

Shot 13 (00:26 – 00:29)
Reprise of pan shot to the grey male spectators, who appear hypnotized, possessed.
or army on earth. We are one people,

Shot 14 (00:29 – 00:32)
Comprehensive shot on the back of the room. Down the
central aisle, we see a very high archway through which
the blonde woman makes her entrance. Arriving toward
center screen, she slows down. She's going to stop.

with one will,

Shot 15 (00:32 – 00:33)
The black brigade is continuously in pursuit.

one resolve,

Shot 16 (00:33 – 00:37)
Light low-angle shot. Close up on the face of the man on
the screen from the middle of the room.

one cause. Our enemies shall

Shot 17 (00:37 – 00:37)
The blonde woman begins to turn in a circle, swinging
the sledgehammer in her hands.

talk themselves

Shot 18 (00:37 – 00:38)
The black brigade approaches, the vise tightens.

to death

Shot 19 (00:38 – 00:39)
The blonde woman turns faster, with more momentum,
accelerating with the force of a centrifuge.

and we will

Shot 20 (00:39 – 00:41)
Close up of the man on the screen.
                bury them with their own confusion.

Shot 21 (00:41 – 00:43)
The blonde woman completes one final rotation. The
black brigade is almost upon her. In one last effort, with
Olympian desire, she propels the hammer with all her
force by letting out a climactic cry.
                        Arghhhh!

Shot 22 (00:43 – 00:45)
Low-angle shot. The camera follows the hammer that
floats through the space, rotating in slow motion.
                        We shall

Shot 23 (00:45 – 00:46)
Low-angle shot from the middle of the room. We see the
hammer that is about to pierce the middle of the screen.
At the moment it makes contact, the screen explodes in
a white flash of lightning.
                        prevail!

Shot 24 (00:46 – 00:47)
Subjective view of spectators witnessing the explosion.
A blinding light emanates from the screen and nobody
moves.

Shot 25 (00:47 – 00:56)
Shot of the stunned spectators, mouths agape, motionless,

as if petrified. They've taken the blast from the explosion from the front and have been whitened by the dust it's created. The once-still camera now pans from the right to the left.

An off-screen voice reads the following text that appears at center screen:

On January 24th
Apple Computer will introduce
Macintosh.
And you'll see why 1984

Shot 26 (00:56 – 01:00)
Fade out. On the black background appears the Apple logo, the apple in rainbow colors. The voice concludes:

will not be like 1984.

6

THE BIG BROTHER DISCOURSE

One may believe that the Big Brother discourse in the 1984 commercial comes directly from the novel George Orwell published in 1949. That's not so. In *Adweek*, Steve Hayden explains that the production team in London had needed a text to read for casting. Richard O'Neill, the executive producer, put in a phone call. A text was needed as soon as possible. Steve Hayden met his brother David for lunch that day. They amused themselves by pasting together a few lines from Mussolini and Mao. One hour later, the text is written. Ridley Scott loves it. It may not have been planned that way, but he ends up including it in the final version:

> Today we celebrate the first glorious anniversary of the Information Purification Directives. We have created for the first time in all history a garden of pure ideology, where each worker may bloom, secure from the pests of any contradictory true thoughts. Our Unification of Thoughts is more powerful a weapon than any fleet or army on earth. We are one people, with one will, one resolve, one cause. Our enemies shall talk themselves to death and we will bury them with their own confusion. We shall prevail!

7

WAS GEORGE ORWELL RIGHT?

Jack Shore is born in Kansas, in 1956. His father works on a farm. His mother meets with the Holy Mary Mother of God Society. By the time he's twenty-four years old, he's a salesman at RadioShack. In 1983, Apple invites him to attend the Annual Sales Conference in Honolulu. They offer airfare to Hawaii. It's the first time he takes a plane. From the hotel room's window, he can see the Waikiki Beach. It's autumn, 30 degrees in the shade, the water turquoise. Tomorrow morning at 8am, he has to be in the Emerald Room to listen to a conference about the influence of the mouse on human/machine interfaces. In the afternoon, he'll attend technical demonstrations. The following day, October 23rd, he's at the amphitheater of the Convention Center. Nearly 800 people attend the Steve Jobs speech. To the tune of "What A Feeling", a voice belonging to Irene Carter sings, "Apple is leading the way. We are Apple. All together now. We're making a better today. What a feeling!"

He arrives at the podium in a short-sleeved grey polo shirt. He's clean-shaven, longhaired. He's twenty-eight years old. He begins on an ironic note, introducing himself: "Hi, I'm Steve Jobs." A few laugh across the room. Everyone who's there knows exactly who he is. Without him and Steve Wosniak, the room would be empty, Apple wouldn't exist.

He launches into his attack with a grave tone: "It is 1958. IBM passes up the chance to buy a young, fledgling company that has invented a new technology called xerography. Two years later, Xerox is born and IBM has been kicking themselves ever since."

He continues, always theatrical: "It is ten years later, the late sixties." He speaks of Digital Equipment Corporation, better know as DEC, inventors of the mini-computer featuring PDP-1. IBM dismisses the mini-computer by saying that it's too small to do serious computing and therefore unimportant to their business. DEC grows to become a multi-hundred-million-dollar corporation before IBM finally enters the mini-computer market.

"It is now ten years later, the late seventies. In 1977, Apple, a young, fledgling company on the West coast, invents the Apple II, the first personal computer as we know it today." IBM dismisses this machine as too small to do serious computing and unimportant to their business. (Laughter and applause in the room.) Jobs next enumerates the advances made by Apple. He claims these accomplishments like an actor performing Shakespeare.

1981: Apple II is the most popular personal computer on the market. Apple has become a company worth three hundred million dollars. The corporation possesses the fastest growth trajectory of any company in American business history. "With over 50 competitors vying for a share, IBM enters the personal-computer market in November '81, with the IBM PC."

1983: Apple and IBM have become the two biggest competitors in the industry. Each one sells the equivalent of one billion dollars worth of personal computers. Both will invest more than fifty millions dollars each in research and development, along with another fifty million in television advertising for the year 1984. The market is at full boil. Firms start going bankrupt. Total industry losses surpass the combined profits of Apple and IBM.

Here, the speech takes a dramatic turn along the lines of Othello, Act V: "It is now 1984." It is clear that IBMwants to monopolize the industry. Apple, from now on, is seen as the only company capable of keeping it in check, the only hope for competition. The dealers who've supported IBM now fear a company that wants to dominate and control the future. "They are increasingly and desperately turning back to Apple as the only force that can ensure their future freedom." (Applause.) IBM has decided to turn its attention to finishing off Apple, its last obstacle to industry control. Steve Jobs poses the question: "Will Big Blue dominate the entire computer industry, the entire information age?" Numerous voices, in a general wave of disapproval, start calling out, "No! No! No!" Jobs concludes, before a room now in the palm of his hand, with the question, "Was George Orwell right about 1984?" As he utters these words, the lights dim. The waves of applause almost drown out the modulations of a siren. On the giant screen behind him begins the first public presentation of the 1984 commercial.

Jack Shore is electrified. He feels his wings growing. He's in complete agreement with Steve Jobs. They can't leave everything to IBM. Once he's back in Kansas, he's going to put all his efforts behind Apple. There's no time to think it through. He's at the movies in front of a science-fiction movie. The sound at maximum volume surges to a deafening roar of siren modulations. He sees some sort of slave formation walking in line. He sees a blonde woman, running policemen, Big Brother on the screen, the slaves again, the woman approaching, the police behind her, a room. She enters the room, a hammer in her hand. In her white T-shirt and red shorts, she bursts across the screen. In this black-and-white setting, she shines. At the moment of "We will prevail!" the screen explodes. The astonished slaves are now liberated. When the off-screen voice says, "On January 24th, Apple Computer will introduce Macintosh", a huge wave of applause begins to engulf the room, "... and you'll see why 1984 will not be like 1984."

The audience has reached a near-delirious state. The lights come back on. Steve Jobs is still standing at the podium, all his triumph hidden behind a curling smile. They're cheering. They're punching their fists in the air. They're on their feet. Jack slaps the back of his neighbor to the right. He shouts to his neighbor on the left: "Fantastic!" The applause gains even more momentum. Faced with such rousing success, even Jobs is speechless. He relishes the moment. All he can do is raise his thumb in a sign of approval. He's beyond satisfied. The ovation continues for a long time.

That day, Jack and his peers don't pick up on the strange similitude that exists between the mute zombies of the commercial and themselves, the hysterical salesmen in the Honolulu Convention Center.

8

LOREM IPSUM

After being back home for a week, Jack Shore falls asleep in front of the TV. There was a special on the next Olympic Winter Games in Sarajevo. Prior to that evening, he's never heard of the place. What he's really interested in are the games that'll happen in Los Angeles that summer.

He's woken up by the intro music of a Bugs Bunny cartoon, a Warner Brothers production. Merrie Melodies. REG. U.S. PAT. OFF. (Registered with the United States Patent Office).

Produced by Leon Schlesinger in Technicolor.

WACKIKI WABBIT

Supervision: Charles M. Jones

Animation: Ken Harris

Story: Tedd Pierce

Musical Direction: Carl W. Stalling

The title of the Bugs Bunny episode makes Jack chuckle. It takes him back to Hawaii. He never would have believed that one day he'd see Waikiki Beach. He hadn't ever imagined himself kicking up the mythical sands of

American surfers. That's where Duke Kahanamoku got started. He's begun to regret having missed his chance to visit Pearl Harbor when Bugs Bunny sets himself up as Tarzan. He throws himself at a vine and imitates the nasally cry of the Ape Man. Jack laughs. He loves Bugs Bunny. In the next scene, the rabbit is dressed up as a Hawaiian. He impersonates the islands' dialect. There are subtitles. They say, "Now is the time for every good man to come to the aid of his party." When you look up what that passage means, you see that it's actually a phrase used in certain methods of typing. It dates from 1918 and was first written by Frank McGurrin, an expert in the speed of the first Remingtons. With time, the phrase developed a life of its own as dummy text, a lorem ipsum.

9

ON THE KEY

Once, the command keys of Apple keyboards featured an apple and a sort of square with looped corners (a Bowen knot). Next to the space bar, there was a key with this: . By pressing this key and the "S" key together, you could save an open document. With time, we got in the habit of saying that in order to save you had to press "Apple S". In 2007, the apple was replaced by the letters c, m, and d. To save, we now have to press "Command S". In any event, Apple is still the key.

MAURICE RICHARD

He comes into the world the year Einstein and James Dean depart. It's 1955. At the Academy Awards, *On the Waterfront* wins best picture, best director (Elia Kazan), and best actor (Marlon Brando). Vladimir Nabokov publishes Lolita. Richard Brautigan leaves Oregon for San Francisco. Lee Meriwether, the first Catwoman to appear in a Batman film, is named Miss America. In Montgomery, Alabama, Rosa Parks refuses to sit at the back of a bus, the beginning of a movement for civil rights continued by Martin Luther King.

In the spring of 1955, Clarence Campbell, the president of the National Hockey League, suspends Maurice Richard. The Canadien's star player had bodychecked a linesman. The man dubbed The Rocket doesn't finish the season. On March 17, during a game at the Montreal Forum, a dispute between spectators and Campbell over the severity of the punishment explodes into a riot. Quebeckers unleash their anger in the face of what they consider yet another injustice. The English have once again pushed down the French Canadians. The defeat at the Plains of Abraham still burns within them. In the streets they set fires, damage cars and shops, carry signs that read "Campbell the English pig", "Richard the persecuted". They revolt against the empire. According to some, this is the event that marks the beginning of the Québécois revolution otherwise qualified as Quiet.

Steve Jobs arrives in the world the year the Montreal Canadiens lose the Stanley Cup to the Detroit Red Wings. The next year, Maurice Rocket Richard, Jean Béliveau, and Doug Harvey win it for Montreal. It's seen as revenge for an entire nation.

When he spoke to me about Maurice Richard, my father had a glimmer in his eyes that made me want to become a hockey player.

11

CONTRACTIONS

Yesterday, Annie-Anne had
her first contractions.
These final gasps
for what comes next.

12

REGENCY TR-1

In the April 1955 edition of Consumer Reports, an entire page is dedicated to the TR-1. It is the brand-new transistor radio from Regency. The radio's big novelty is its size. It's the smallest radio in the world. It can fit in a pocket. The TR-1 is significant because it's the first widely available electronic device that uses transistors instead of electronic tubes.

According to Consumer Reports, the transistor is one of the biggest technological advances of the first half of the twentieth century. It carries the promise of major revolutions in the domain of communications. The advantages of transistors over empty tubes are numerous. They're tiny, practically the size of a match head. They radiate very little heat. They require only a little voltage. In theory, their lifespan is unlimited.

Under the watchful eye of his wife, Paul Jobs delicately tears open the red and green wrapping paper of his gift box. When he discovers that her Christmas present to him is a Regency TR-1, the world's smallest radio, he gets up and plants a kiss on her forehead. She cradles in her arms their ten-month-old adopted son, Steven Paul Jobs.

Same shape, same wheel adjuster, forty-six years later
the design of the first Apple iPod strangely recalls that of
the first Regency TR-1

13

BENCHMARKING

He works in a marketing department. Most of his colleagues come from business school. He launches new products into the marketplace and evaluates existing lines. At twenty years old, he drives a Volkswagen. At thirty years old, he drives a BMW. Soon after the kids, he needs a big Jeep to drive them all around. They measure their happiness by the size of their television, by the power of their computers and the whiteness of their teeth. The further they travel on vacations, be it huts on stilts in the Pacific, five-star hotels in the mountains of Cambodia, the more they have the sensation of existing. That dad is a doctor, mom a pharmacist, that their grandfather is the former president of the Chamber of Commerce, none of that has anything to do with their success. They believe nothing can be credited to their origins. They are simply better than others.

He works in a marketing department. It could be bearable without his colleagues. Their market studies, their benchmarking, their SWOT analyses, their Excel spreadsheets, their business lunches and their PowerPoint presentations aren't sufficient enough to cover their vacuity.

They think they're all Steve Jobs in the making. He watches as they scurry along. It makes him sick. He would like to be a believer, it would be simpler.

Benchmarking consists of studying the best practices of competitive forces and then innovating or copying them.

He no longer works in a marketing department and Steve Jobs is dead.

14

1984

In 1984, Johnny Weissmuller dies of old age. Richard Brautigan fires a bullet into his head, and Gabriel Rivages loses his virginity. It's also the year Apple launches Macintosh.

15

WRONG TRACK

He follows his route back. He drives back up to San Francisco Bay. He recrosses under the Golden Gate, the bridge that gets its name from the Gold Rush. On the opposite shore, he conjures up Monterey, San Luis Obispo, Los Angeles and Tijuana. He leaves Mexico to his left, skips over the Panama Canal. He feels the offshore winds coming in from Peru and, beyond that, Chile. At the furthest tips of the Tierra del Fuego, he crosses the straits just as Magellan did in 1520. The way is long, across the middle of the Atlantic, toward Gibraltar. He keeps his course. Like Hercules before him, the Mediterranean carries him toward the Orient. At the port of Tripoli, his destination is almost in sight. Several days of walking, a caravan, camels, a well, the black eyes of a mysterious woman. She reminds him of Erina. After travelling halfway around the world, after seasickness and nightmares, he reaches Homs. He stands before a Crusader castle in Syria, the Krak des Chevaliers. He's traced back his path, in reverse. He's seen whales in the open seas of Montevideo. Dolphins dancing off the coast of Malta.

Because he wanted to understand, he had to follow the footsteps of his father, born in Homs, Syria. Because he wanted to understand, he traversed the globe. Driven to search, he almost lost himself. He found nothing in Homs. He'd retraced his father's journey in reverse and found nothing. The castle on the mountain, there since the time of the crusades, offered him no reprieve. Homs is a city of the Middle East. Homs is a city like all the others. Abdulfattah Jandali is a man like all the others. Born around 1930, he emigrated to the United States. He settled down in California. Apart from that, he's the biological father of Steve Jobs. And so? He's born in Homs, he emigrated to the United States, and he never knew his son. His son never wanted to know him. The path offered by origins is occasionally the wrong track.

THE APPLE NEVER FALLS FAR
FROM THE TREE

Pomona, goddess of fruit
Falling with apples
Apple pie
Apple of my eye
Adam's apple
Bad apple
The Big Apple
An apple for the road
An apple a day
Apples and oranges
Pineapple
The apple never falls far from the tree

IRON MAIDEN

On November 26, 1984, we went to see the Iron Maiden concert at the Colisée de Québec. It was for the World Slavery Tour. At one point, Eddy, the group's monster mascot, unscrews his skull and removes his brain. The crowd goes wild. This real heavy metal for misunderstood teens, full of complexes and acne, strikes a chord. We have nothing else but music that expresses our anger.

At the beginning of his book *The Sleepwalkers*, Arthur Koestler explains that it was music that gave birth to mathematics and science as we conceive them:

> The Pythagorean discovery that the pitch of a note depends on the length of the string which produces it, and that concordant intervals in the scale are produced by simple numerical ratios (2:1 octave, 3:2 fifth, 4:3 fourth, etc.), was epoch-making: it was the first successful reduction of quality to quantity, the first step towards the mathematization of human experience—and therefore the beginning of Science.

It's no doubt because of this that many great scientists

are excellent musicians. The language of music and the language of mathematics are similar, speaking to us without words. Einstein played the violin.

In our French course, in Grade 11, we had to make a diaporama. We chose the atomic bomb as our subject. On one of the slides, you see the famous photo of the nuclear mushroom cloud, taken by Sergeant Bob Caron after Little Boy was dropped on Hiroshima. Stationed in the back of the *Enola Gay,* he is the only person to have witnessed from the sky that most destructive explosion in the history of humanity. That was August 6, 1945. To emphasize the apocalyptic aspect of what we showed, we included an Iron Maiden guitar solo as its soundtrack. How had humanity, with its science, arrived at this point? We have but music to express our anger. And Einstein played the violin.

ADAM'S APPLE

God doesn't really have more than one bastard. Think about it for two minutes. He created man and woman in his image. He arranged for them to live in the midst of a marvelous garden where all is beautiful, serene, and symbiotic. It's a paradise. All is for the better in the best of worlds, and that can last forever. But look how he plants, right in the middle of the garden, a tree upon which is written: do not touch. It's really sleazy. He could have easily planted his tree of knowledge elsewhere. He could have fenced it off with barbed wire jutted with razors, like at Guantanamo. Instead, he places his tree right where everyone can behold it. He made it grow the strange fruit of Creation. He goes to see Adam and Eve to tell them that they can do anything they please, except eat the fruit from the tree of good and evil.

We know what happens next. The snake shows up. It seduces Eve. She bites into the apple and shares it with Adam. They realize, then, that they are both naked. God is enraged. He chases them out of paradise and promises them the worst suffering.

What's funny about this story is that nowhere in the Bible is the fruit in question specified as an apple. The text only describes the fruit of a tree that possesses the knowledge of good and evil. Who decided that it would be an apple? In any case, we say that Adam, as a result of this story, is left with the fruit stuck in his throat. That's why, in men, the growth of thyroid cartilage is called an Adam's apple.

19

MATHEMATICS

What is a trilogy? It's proof by four that there can never be two without three.

20

APRIL FOOL'S

Originally, it's spelled: iota, khi, theta, upsilon, sigma. In Ancient Greek, ichtus means fish. In Roman, it corresponds to the first letters of the following five words: Iêsos Christos Theou Uios Sôtèr (ictus). It means: Jesus Christ, son of God, Savior. That's how the fish became the symbol of Christ. For Rivages, this all reminds him of his grandmother. She always had the same bumper sticker on her car. It was a sticker in the shape of a fish with Jesus written across it. His grandmother attended mass every Sunday. She never knew that the fish related back to the Greeks. What does that change anyways? Nothing, but Rivages can't help but uncover origin stories when he wants to understand.

Not much is known about the origins of the April Fool's tradition. Why do we tell tall tales on that day? Why do we play tricks? Why do we tape paper fish on people's backs It could connect back to the Zodiac. This would have come about at the time that the Sun rose from the sign of Pisces. There's also a story that speaks of the end of Lent. Others say that to celebrate the Annunciation people gave presents on the first day of April. They commemorated the day that the Archangel Gabriel tells Mary she's pregnant.

Apple is officially founded on April 1, 1976. April Fool's Day. Steve Jobs and Steve Wozniak own ninety percent of the business. The remaining ten percent belongs to Ron Wayne. He's the one who draws the company's first logo with Newton sitting under an apple tree. But two weeks later, Ron changes his mind. He regrets jumping into this adventure. He doesn't believe in it. Anyways, he doesn't like the idea of founding a company on April Fool's Day. He sees it as a bad omen. He sells his shares back to the two Steves for eight hundred dollars. Thirty years later, they're valued at three billion. Ever since April 1, 1976, Ron Wayne has the impression that a permanent paper fish has been pasted to his back.

21

WHITE PAGE

At seven years old. Rivages is lousy at French. He mixes up his p's and b's, his m's and n's, his v's and f's, among other things. His father owns Elpis Vresley records. There's a batio door in the living room. While the rest of the class takes catechism lessons, he takes a speech adjustment course. A woman helps him sort out the letters in his head. With time, he gets there. He's good at composition but average in spelling. He uses the language well, all while flouting its rules.

At twenty years old, he buys a Macintosh computer. As a bonus, he buys spelling-correction software. Thanks to the machine and the software, he can finally write an entire page without making errors. He can finally overcome his fear of writing. Without his first Mac and the Corrector 101, he would forever be stuck on a white page.

22

MYTHOLOGY

Zeus beds with Semele. Dionysos is their son.

Zeus beds with Leda. She delivers the beautiful Helen and Clytemnestra.

Zeus beds with Metis. Athena is their daughter.

Zeus beds with Leto, who gives birth to Artemis and Apollo.

Zeus beds with Maia to give life to Hermes.

Zeus beds with Pluto and conceives Tantalus.

Zeus beds with Selene, who delivers Pandia and Ersa.

Zeus beds with Mnemosyne, Calyce, Io, Europa, Danaë, Alcmene, Electra, etc.

The Greek myths are pretty much always sex stories.

23

SNOW WHITE

In *Annie Hall*, Woody Allen recounts the story of how, the day his mother took him to see *Snow White and the Seven Dwarfs*, he understands that he's different. All the children fall in love with Snow White, except for him. He prefers the wicked queen dressed in black. For Gabriel, it's a revelation. Finally someone who has the courage to say out loud what he's kept secret since he was seven. Finally someone who understands this youthful titillation experienced at the sight of the queen before she transforms herself into a witch.

Rumor has it that Alan Turing committed suicide by biting into an apple poisoned with cyanide in homage to the *Snow White* movie which he loved. Born in 1912, he's sixteen when he reads and understands Einstein's work. Upon its release, children were not permitted to see the Disney movie! Turing, one of the fathers of computing, dies on June 7, 1954.

Inspired by the Brothers Grimm fairy tale, Walt Disney's *Snow White* comes out in 1937. Now that he knows that it was Joan Crawford who personified the queen, Gabriel better understands his childhood excitement. On the other hand, he also now knows that the song "Heigh-ho, Heigh-ho, it's home from work we go" is inspired by a Nazi song, so he no longer whistles it while working.

24

THE ROOF OF THE WORLD

He's now been alive for sixty hours and thirty-nine minutes. He's a boy. This evening before leaving, Rivages changes his son's diaper. The midwife showed him how to do it: unfasten the diaper, hold the two feet up high in one hand, remove the diaper, clean, replace with a clean diaper, hook it… That's a good poo poo. From now on, Rivages belongs to that group of people who revel over the contents of a baby's diaper. It's a thrill, apart from the smell. Baby drinks a lot of milk for the first two days. You have to wonder where all that liquid goes. The mystery of digestion. But all is going well, and changing a diaper brings happiness because of the contact it provides. He sees his son better. He gazes at him up-close. He can feel him, smell him. He's experiencing one of life's big moments. Rivages wonders if this is what Herzog experienced upon reaching the summit of Annapurna. His son is not even three days old and he's already on top of the world.

25

RADAR

The first time he hears the name Norbert Wiener, Rivages is in a communications theory course. It's about the message, the emitter, the receiver, noise and feedback (retroaction). Enrolled in university, all Rivages wants is to become a journalist. All this is a bit vague. The concept of feedback is explained and he's given an example of a toilet flushing. It's an auto-regulating mechanism. Once the bowl is empty, a float indicates to the mechanism that it needs to be refilled. The system auto-regulates thanks to an exchange of information, messages.

Norbert Wiener is born in 1894, in Missouri. A child prodigy, he enters university at the age of eleven. His interests include logic, zoology, and philosophy. At eighteen, he obtains a doctorate in mathematics from Harvard. During the Second World War, he works on the development of anti-aircraft missiles. For the missile to strike its target accurately, he must be able to adjust its trajectory according to the location of its target. To make this adjustment, he would require information that, in this case, can only be provided to him by radar. As a result of his research for the American military, Wiener forges his theory of communication. His concepts are adopted in psychology, biology, economics, computer science and numerous other disciplines.

The second time Rivages encounters Wiener is in literature. Wiener is the father of cybernetics, and cybernetics have influenced a lot of people during the second half of the twentieth century, among them many writers. And not only authors like Philip K. Dick; a guy like Richard Brautigan in 1967 wrote a very nice poem on the subject: "All Watched Over by Machines of Loving Grace." Cybernetics, which is the science of systems, is very much in fashion during the sixties. Wiener's book from 1948, Cybernetics: Or Control and Communication in the Animal and the Machine, is a big success.

The third time Rivages encounters Wiener is in his Steve Jobs novel. He wanted to explain the mathematician's place in the history of computing; its links to the first computers capable of calculating ballistic trajectories. He wanted to articulate everything we owe to Wiener regarding our comprehension of the relations between man and machine. He wished to give an account of this genius's body of work. But he can't. He realizes that he doesn't have the ability to do so. He has neither the intelligence nor the talent. It's too late. At forty years old, all that he can bring himself to say is that the word radar is a palindrome. It's taken from the first letters of RAdio Detection And Ranging.

26

CHOSEN

Steve Jobs' story begins with his adoption. For psychologists, his success in the business world is rooted in this first trauma. Rejected by his original parents, the child must have developed a strong need to be I don't know if that's how things go.

I don't know at what age Steve learns he's adopted. Apparently, he was still a child at the time. I ask myself how I'd react to this news at age seven. It's true that, generally, it means that at the beginning someone decided that they did not want you. Unless your parents are dead. In that case, it's different, and you're an orphan.

I wonder what a child understands when we tell him that he has adoptive parents. For him, whether they're adoptive or biological, what does it change? What are the impacts of genetic links upon our lives?

Apparently, Steve's adoptive parents explain to him that his real parents could not keep him. They tell him, "We got to choose you. You can look at life from two sides. You can think for your whole life that you were abandoned, or you can think for your whole life that you were chosen."

27

MY NEIGHBOR

Like my neighbor says, "Nobody is like everyone else."

28

ADA

There will be a woman who will bed with a man. At the foot of the mountain, they will make love on a mattress on the floor. Nothing but their bare feet will be seen from behind the rice-paper wall. She will be draped in silk. After making love, the man will show her a book. She will serve him tea. The wind will rustle the bamboo leaves. The book will tell the woman that she should leave. The book will tell the woman that she should walk. The book will tell the woman to follow the setting sun.

She will go. She will walk, cross the mountains and meet other men, other women. A child will grow in her enlarged belly. She will reach the desert. The child will grow up. The woman will die. The child will guard the book. An adult, he will translate the book for his people in the desert. Amidst scents of spice and mint, they will go to hear him read from the book. The book will say, "Only perseverance can overcome slow progress without getting lost in the sand." Ten centuries later, nothing will be left of the child. Only the book will remain.

Then the son of the son of all the other sons across the centuries will happen to write another book. Men will come from very far away. They will give him gold and horses. They will return to their countries with his book and many others. Over there, men will discover his book. They will understand its power. They will be fascinated. They will undergo revelatory experiences. The discovery of Al-Khwarizmi's algebra and the use of zero will be, for them, like the dawn of a new era. From within the depths of the Córdoba Castle, the rumors of a new science will take root.

It will take a few more centuries before these new discoveries cross the Channel and conquer England. It will have to wait several more centuries for Lord Byron to become a father to Ada Lovelace. It will be another wait for the first encounter between Ada and Babbage but, one day, it will exist, the first computer program in the history of humanity. One day, the first algorithm written to be executed by a machine will exist. Nothing will be left of the woman from the mountains of the Far East. All that will remain is the name of the daughter of an English poet. All that will remain is Ada, the name of a computer language developed for the American military in the twentieth century.

FREE FALLING

He doesn't know what he's getting into. He doesn't know where he's going. It's stronger than him. He must know how to leap. He must leap. The Cessna is at an altitude of three thousand meters. The pilot cuts the motor. The instructor opens the door. They gather under the wing of the plane. Standing on a simple step, they grip the crossbar. The motion was repeated ten times that morning: "Ready, set, go." At "go", he must let it all go. "Ready, set, go" and release. From an altitude of three thousand meters, the fall begins. In a second, the Cessna is already far away. It's a void, more a nothing than anything he can cling to. Impossible to go back, they take a big leap. They tumble in a ball before sprawling out their legs and arms. In a first movement, as if by reflex, they curl up, a fetal position. The body's fears have spoken. They must stretch out their arms and legs. They motion was repeated ten times that morning. The fall stabilizes. They slide, stomachs to the wind, bodies facing the ground. The speed plugs our ears. A feeling of complete openness. A combination of patience and urgency. There's no question of getting there, but he can't forget to pull the lever that opens the parachute. He must watch the altimeter. Once the needle quivers into the yellow zone, he must pull on the handle.

The parachute escapes. They feel absolutely nothing. It's amazing. In movies, you always get the impression that you'll be greeted with a great jolt. That it would feel brutal. Not at all; all of a sudden, they find themselves simply upright. They float, feet dangling in emptiness, attached to a sheet several square meters wide. After a free fall of thirty seconds, they are halfway between the plane and the ground. They will now float for five minutes. They will admire the view. They will forget that the smallest technical problem could result in assured death. The descent is gentle, the sensation obviously one of flight. A cord in each hand, they turn left by pulling right and turn right by pulling left.

At the moment of touching down, they pull on both cords at the same time. It's like jumping off a table. The impact is no more violent than that. The movement was repeated ten times that morning. Returning to solid ground is an awkward feeling. They stumble. They are dizzy. The body overflows with adrenaline. For two or three days, the sensation continues to live on in us, stronger than us. Once on the ground, it's hard to remain on earth.

23 HOURS, 28 MINUTES & 666 VIRGINS

Twenty-three hours and twenty-eight minutes, at times, that can really feel depressing. It's as if, between now and twenty-three hours and twenty-eight minutes, as many centuries have come and gone as between me and Tutankhamen up on a massive golden chariot pulled by six hundred and sixty-six virgins.

UNTIL FUXI

Sitting on the ground, Fuxi enters the void. Legs folded, he braces himself in an upright pose. Eyes open, he fixates on the horizon. Concentrated on himself, he observes the world. The sun rises, the night disappears. The sun sets, the night returns. Body on the ground, he directs his head to the sky. He knows he has a father and a mother. He knows the seasons and the movements of the heart. We are in China, five thousand years ago. This observation of the world in its duality, in its contrasts, in its complements, is the base of Oriental philosophy. It's deployed in the concepts of yin and yang. The taijitu is its symbol. We see two fish interlocked in a circle. The white fish has a black eye. The black fish has a white eye.

The void and plenitude, the long and short, truth and untruth, are states. They can be represented by two signs, in a binary manner. By combining these signs, new symbols are created. It's this principle of Bagua's eight trigrams that, according to Chinese myth, are the basis of Fuxi's work. The trigrams are broken and unbroken lines grouped in threes:

☰ ☷ ☳ ☴ ☵ ☶ ☶ ☱

These symbols represent the sky, earth, thunder, wind, fire, water, mountains, marshland. The express equally all the possible combinations of two symbols grouped in threes. There are eight possibilities in total. In mathematics, it's written as 2^3, which is to say 2 x 2 x 2, which equals 8. If we decide to group these symbols in packs of four (2^4), we obtain sixteen different results. If we continue: $2^5 = 32$, $2^6 = 64$, $2^7 = 128$, $2^8 = 256$, $2^9 = 512$, $2^{10} = 1024$, $2^{11} = 2048$, etc. In computing, this suite of numbers comes up often, since a computer can only recognize two symbols, the 0 and the 1.

The concept of yin and yang is a manner of stripping back the world to its simplest expression. Fuxi's eight trigrams are a manner of representing decimal numbers from 1 to 8 using only two symbols. Five thousand years ago, the world became a binary. For this reason, the history of computing usually goes back all the way to Fuxi.

32

ORIGIN

The mother
of her mother
died the other day.

She says
that a grandmother
is childhood.

33

FIAT LUX

Thomas Edison does not invent the electric light bulb. That's two Canadians, Henry Woodward and Matthew Evans, who are first to make a metallic wire burn in a tube of glass. Their patent, # 3738, dates from July 24, 1874.

Thomas Edison does not invent the electric light bulb; he invents the modern laboratory. In 1876, at Menlo Park, in New Jersey, he sets up a factory to build inventions. He knows that an idea, no matter how good, is nothing if it can't be sold. He buys patent #3738 and asks his teams to improve it. It needs to be a simple product, clear, durable, easy to make and to use. At Menlo Park, they work on it for five years. The risk is worth the reward. The electric light bulb sees the light of day. Thomas Alva Edison lights up the world. It's the birth of General Electric.

Edison doesn't invent the electric light bulb; he commercializes it. In the same manner, Jobs doesn't invent the personal computer; he determines its best course to market. Given these similarities, saying that Steve Jobs is the Thomas Edison of the twentieth century isn't really an exaggeration.

As a result of observing electric light bulbs, Edison remarks that with time, the top of the bulb blackens. He concludes that invisible elements escape the filament when heated to whiteness. He has a point. Electrons escape, which go on to stain the glass. Today, this phenomenon still carries the name of the man who observed it for the first time: the Edison effect.

This observation triggered a stream of scientific research. Little by little, year after year, men and women conducted experiments to try to understand an invisible world. They came up with hypotheses on massless particles charged with electricity, electrons, and a nucleus where the positive charge maintains electrons in orbit.

People came to realize that the infinitely small was made in the image of the infinitely large; that the atomic world had its own sun and planets. They found the means to excite electrons in a manner and control them, to guide them. The first street lights weren't even fifty years old when the atomic bomb was invented in Los Alamos. Microwaves and computers followed the same pathways. As research continued, technicians were able to put in place a regulatory system for the movement of electrons in glass tubes, the bulbs of the first TV sets. When the transistor arrived, it was little more than a bold miniaturization of the Edison effect. The computer is the child of the transistor, and the great-great-great-grandchild of the electric light bulb.

34

TI 99/4A

He wanted a motorbike, but he got a computer. His father
wanted him to take an interest in micro-computing. In
1982, that was the beginning of the future. That's how
one Saturday morning, he managed to connect a Texas
Instruments TI 99/4A to the black-and-white TV in the
living room. For the computer to do anything, it needed
a program using the language Basic. The first example
he was given in the instruction manual resembled this:

```
10 REM First try
20 CLS
30 PRINT "Hello."
40 INPUT "What is your name?"; name$
50 PRINT "Welcome" + name$
60 END
```

When the program launched at the typing of the
word RUN, the results on the screen were close to that:

COMPUTER: Hello.
What is your name?

HUMAN: Gabriel [*enter*]
COMPUTER: Hello Gabriel

It subtly gave the impression of talking to the machine. It was like assisting in a magic trick while knowing how it worked.

Texas Instruments starts up in Dallas in 1951. It takes place in Texas because, since its beginnings, the company has manufactured detection tools for the petroleum industry. In Texas, there's a lot of oil. And as the products evolve the company obtains sizeable contracts with the military. In 1959, Jack Kilby, an engineer with the company, applies for a patent for the first integrated circuit in the world. But Robert Noyce of the Fairchild Semiconductor Corporation has also invented the first integrated circuit in the world. It's not rare that experts arrive at the same big discovery at the same time. After negotiations, the two companies are in the running to dominate a market worth thousands of billions of dollars.

As for Gabriel, he regretted owning a Texas Instruments for two reasons. Soon, the company would suddenly abandon the manufacturing of personal computers. Also, all his friends had Commodore Vic-20s and their video games weren't compatible with his machine. What he'd wanted all along was a motorbike.

35

HELIOGABALUS

In Germany between the two world wars, the Shiebles decide to leave it all behind for America. They settle along the far side of Lake Michigan, along the west coast, in Wisconsin. The Great Depression keeps them from believing too firmly in the future. Their girl, Joanne, enters the world in 1932. She says her prayers at the side of her bed, her knees on the ground, morning and night. She confesses her sins. She follows the right path. The Schiebles are proud of their daughter. Before every meal, they thank the Lord. When Joanne enters university, her father congratulates her. He's proud of the rigorous education his daughter received. He's proud of having worked hard and of being able to pay for her studies.

One day, Joanne comes home and announces to her parents that she's going on a trip to Syria with a Muslim. Her father sees red. Her mother holds him back. The father reminds her that if she doesn't marry a good Catholic, she can kiss her family and heritage goodbye.

Joanne meets Abdulfattah at university. She had never known a gaze more profound, a face as penetrating. They become lovers. He wants her to meet his family, over there, in Homs. In the plane, he tells her of the cult of the Sun and of the boulder dedicated to it. He recounts for her the legend of the rock, the black boulder. The Roman emperor Heliogabalus is born in Homs during the third century. He's seen as the son of the Sun. The plane passes through some turbulence. He reassures her. All will be well during their trip. His father is a man of wealth and generous spirit. All will be well.

All goes so well that, upon their return, Joanne is pregnant. Her religion forbids abortion. Her father forbids marriage. The only option left is adoption or difficult beginnings for herself and the child. She hears of a doctor who can take care of everything in San Francisco. Before the birth-control pill, there were many doctors who could take care of it all. She takes a plane at the beginning of February. It's 1955. She's put up in a nice room. She's told it's for the recovery afterward. All will go well.

On February 24, 1955, she gives birth to a boy. When the nurse places the baby in her arms, she bursts into tears. How could she do such a thing? However, if her father learns that she had a child, it would be terrible. She prefers the punishment of her motherhood to her father's despair.

A few days later, Paul and Clara Jobs adopt the son of Joanne Schieble and Abdulfattah Jandali. They become the parents of a child conceived in Homs, the birthplace of Heliogabalus. Steve Jobs is, in his way, the son of the Sun. It's made me think that I should absolutely read Antonin Artaud's *Heliogabalus: or, the Crowned Anarchist.*

36

UPDATE

I just turned on my computer. A notification appears on the screen:

New software(s) available for your computer.

Do I want to update Quick Time and iTunes?

Frankly, I don't fucking care.

37

SIMPLICITY

If Steve Wozniak and Steve Jobs want to launch a company, they need a name. As the story goes, one day as they were driving around in Jobs's VW, he proposed "Apple" because he'd just come back from spending his summer in Oregon, working in an orchard. It's said that, during this period, Jobs practiced certain forms of asceticism and meditation. He's known for eating nothing more than apples for entire weeks. Also, Jobs considered it a good name because, in the telephone directory, their company would be listed before Atari.

Several years later, an Apple engineer is put in charge of a new development project. He needs to name the project. His goal is to build a more efficient computer. Since he works at Apple, he chooses the name of a variety of apple well known in the United States: the McIntosh.

John McIntosh settles in Hamilton, Ontario, at the beginning of the nineteenth century. Because he transplants an apple tree and his sons know how to make a business flourish, the McIntosh becomes the bestselling apple in America. An apple a day keeps the doctor away. Because John transplants a tree in Ontario at the beginning of the nineteenth century, millions of people own a Mac. Apple had to change the original spelling for legal reasons.

Even so, it was an inspired idea for a company name: Apple. Simply one word, but one that carries within it stories of gods, of the world's creation, of original sin and of awareness. For Jobs, the computer is an instrument of knowledge, a tool for learning, for becoming more intelligent, so he chose the biggest symbol of this quest: the fruit of knowledge. As time passed, Jobs would view himself a little in God's image, or at least his son. A story goes that he once attended a Halloween party disguised as Jesus Christ.

Apple. It couldn't have been any simpler than that. If Jobs is the real father of Apple, it's above all because he baptized it. Today, when we google "Apple", no more fruit appears; all that remains is the company.

38

THE ART OF SPEAKING

Hello, yes, I'm about to get on the plane.
I'm in Bordeaux.
I'll call you back after landing.

Hello, yes, we've just landed.
I'm in Paris.
I'll pick up my luggage and call you back.

Yes, hello, I'm in the taxi.
I'll call you once I get there.

Hello, yes, it's quite the traffic jam.
I don't know if I'll get there on time.
I'll call you back.

Yes, hello, just to let you know,
I might not be able to call you back,
The battery of my iPhone is almo…

39

ATTRACTIONS

The truth is that an apple never fell on Isaac Newton's head. The truth is that Newton was a bit of an alchemist, and a bit of a mystic. The truth is, the day he understood that an invisible force could pull one body to the other, he still didn't believe what had happened. In the end, he was convinced because his calculations confirmed it. The trajectory of the Earth around the Sun corroborated his theory. But how to explain this force? What was it? He calls it attraction, gravitation. He notes that terrestrial mass attracts objects, small and large: an apple, a man, the Moon. There exists between two masses an invisible force that relates them. It is expressed in meters by squared seconds. On Earth, that force is 9.8 m/s2. Newton waited many years before talking about this force. He believed people would think he was crazy. He was convinced of its existence ever since he could calculate its effects. But he couldn't define nor explain it clearly. By studying the problem of attraction, Einstein completes his theory of relativity that, however narrow, is accepted generally. Gravitation would be a deformation in space-time. Nevertheless, even today, the nature of gravitational force remains an impenetrable mystery, one that quantum physics is still trying to pierce.

In 1976, Apple's first logo is a drawing in black and white. Isaac Newton reads a book under an apple tree. The apple is there, menacingly about to fall on his head. One year later, Steve Jobs wants a real logo. Rob Janoff creates an apple in the colors of the rainbow. So that no one would confuse it for a tomato, he draws a bite in it. It's said that Jobs found the whole apple looked like a cherry. The bitten apple recalls the fruit of knowledge. No apple had ever been bitten before Eve. It's the first mistake and the beginning of our humanity. In the Old Testament, the rainbow marks the alliance with God after the flood. In Chinese myth, the rainbow appears at the birth of Fuxi. Newton is the first to explain how white light constitutes a mix of all the colors in a rainbow.

Often in life, there are attractions that we cannot explain. We can only witness them.

40

EMPTY BOTTLES

On June 24, 1984, I turned fifteen years old and was finally allowed to sleep along the riverbank on Saint-Jean-Baptiste Day. At midnight, they lit a bonfire. I was with Nelson, Martin, and Christian, and we were already drunk. That's how I met her. I asked her for a beer. She was drinking Löwenbräu. She was, without a doubt, the only person drinking German beer the night of Quebec's national holiday. I've long kept the cap of that beer as a souvenir of our first kiss. There was a picture of a dragon on it. We went home as the sun rose. It was my first time staying up all night. With Nelson, we collected empty bottles for two hours. We had so many that we used our sleeping bags to carry them all. We looked pretty strange transporting those funny bags on our mopeds, but we each made thirty dollars.

I called her back the next day. It was summer. We were fifteen. During the day, my job was to pick vegetables. In the evening, we kissed with our tongues. We walked, and we kissed. Between desire and fear, we became adults. Toward the end of the summer, we decided to do it. It wasn't a success, but it was done. One month later, we broke up. From the Saint-Jean bonfire, all that remained were embers. I was fifteen years old, Steve Jobs twenty-nine. As he reaped his first millions, I made myself thirty dollars off empty bottles.

41

FIVE-VOLUME *LAROUSSE* FULL-COLOR DICTIONARY (1977)

Computer noun. A universal arithmetic calculator composed of a variable number of specialized units, directed by a single registered program, and that permits, without human intervention, in the course of its work, to effect complex formulations of arithmetic and logic operations for scientific, administrative, and accounting purposes. (A computer contains: **1.** *Enterable units submitted for treatment*; **2.** *A central unit, containing circuits for calculation, comparison, systematic verification, and logical decision-making, and a command post*; **3.** *Memory*; **4.** *Units to output results.* Computers are used to resolve problems requiring scientific calculation, operational research, or scientific management of a commercial or industrial enterprise.) [Also known as PERSONAL COMPUTER AND MASS ELECTRONIC APPLICATION INFORMATION SYSTEM]♦ computer specialist noun. Person whose job is related to computers (programmer, analyst, etc.).

42

WITH THE TONGUE

He opened the cardboard box. He pulled away the blocks of Styrofoam. He grabbed the handle on the top. With veneration, in a firm upward gesture, he gently liberated the machine. A beige cube presented itself to him, its piercing face a black screen. He experienced in this moment something like the apparition of the monolith at the beginning of *2001: A Space Ody*ssey. It was 1993.

He placed his new Mac on his desk. He consulted the Quick Start manual. He connected the power cable. He connected the keyboard cable to the keyboard outlet, the mouse cable in the mouse outlet. There were also diskettes, a System Installation guide, A funny-looking microphone that didn't look like a microphone, and a sticker in the shape of an apple in the colors of a rainbow.

After having verified everything, read everything, he turned on the apparatus. He heard something like mallet striking a gong. The screen turned grey. At its center appeared an icon of a computer that was smiling. His heart beat like it was its very first time, like the first time he French-kissed a girl.

43

O KO MO GO TO PO EO ZO YO

O $2^0 = 1 = 1$ byte

KO $2^{10} = 1024 = 1$ kilobyte

MO $2^{20} = 1048576 = 1$ megabyte

GO $2^{30} = 1073741824 = 1$ gigabyte

TO $2^{40} = 1099511627776 = 1$ terabyte

PO $2^{50} = 1125899906842624 = 1$ petabyte

EO $2^{60} = 1152921504606847000 = 1$ exabyte

ZO $2^{70} = 1.1805916207174113E+21 = 1$ zettabyte

YO $2^{80} = 1.2089258196146292E+24 = 1$ yottabyte

Byte, kilo, mega, giga, tera, péta, exa, zetta, yotta.

44

HP

This is the story of a twelve-year-old child who participates in an electronics lab. He needs certain components for his project. It's explained to him that the parts are too expensive and hard to find. They have to be ordered from Hewlett-Packard. That's not possible. Since he's driven by nature, the setback doesn't take the wind out of his sails.

In 1967, Bill Hewlett is head of the company he founded in a garage with David Packard. The company has almost ten thousand employees. Bill arrives at the office and reads the *San Francisco Chronicle*. An article about the demonstrations against the Vietnam War enrages him. He pours a scotch. The telephone rings. His secretary says there's a call for him. He takes it. A child explains that he needs certain components for his electronics-lab project. Hewlett is blown away. He's caught off guard by the child's confidence. He shakes his head in disbelief. To recompose himself in the face of such audacity, Bill Hewlett offers the boy the pieces he needs. Before hanging up, Bill tells Steve that, if he needs a summer job, he's welcome at HP.

When Bill Hewlett and Dave Packard start HP in a Palo Alto garage in 1939, it ends up being the beginning of the Silicon Valley story. Their first product is an audio system sold to Disney studios. In 1972, they launch the HP-35 calculator that can be considered the first pocket computer, the first PC in the history of computing.

In the stories he later recounts of his chance phone call with the head of HP, Steve Jobs reinvents his origins. Everything's in place to connect the dots. He'd never known his biological father, but Bill Hewlett took him under his wing.

45

BEST SCORE

After three days in the maternity ward, we're going back home. We sign exit documents at the office. Six pounds and eight ounces wrapped in a bundle for the trip home. Tucked into the bassinet, only the tip of his nose is visible. I go to get the car. We set him into the backseat and ensure that all the snaps are secured correctly. We check them once, twice, three times... Enough checking, we have to hit the road. In traffic, with my three-day-old son in the back, I don't try to pass anyone. It's the first time I've been so afraid driving a car. I feel like I'm in a video game. The game is coming to an end, and I'm about to surpass my best score. There are enemies everywhere, and bombs rain down harder than ever. I use my last life. I have to hold on, I have to hold on.

We've arrived without incident. Our son in our arms, we're introducing him to his home for the first time. It was better than all the best scores in the world.

46

THE HARDER THE FALL

In 1966, Robert Fraser buys a small Magritte painting. It's called *Le jeu de mourre*. It features a big green apple, upon which the words "Au revoir" appear in white cursive script. Fraser is a good friend of Paul McCartney, who loves Magritte's work. One day Fraser drops by for a visit, but McCartney isn't home. As a way of indicating he stopped by to say hello, Fraser asks the maid if he can leave him the painting, which has "Au revoir" written on it in white brushstroke.

McCartney appreciates the gesture. No one has ever said goodbye to him in such an original manner. He buys a frame and hangs it on the wall. Almost half of Magritte's twelve-hundred paintings hang in private collections today. The former Beatle owns twenty-five. The apple from Le jeu de mourre will go on to become the logo for Apple Corps, the company founded by the Beatles. They want to develop experimental sound projects in a context of complete freedom. The third album from Zapple, Apple Corps' record label, is entitled Listening to Richard Brautigan.

The Beatles company and that of Steve Jobs were tied up in court for a long time over the rights to use the brand name "Apple". After years of legal battles, they arrived at a settlement. That's why we can find the Beatles in Apple's iTunes Store, "The group that changed everything."

Magritte's body of work comprises of numerous paintings that have an apple as their principal subject. In the series "La chambre d'écoute" (The Listening Room), a gigantic apple occupies all the space in a room. A famous self-portrait of Magritte has the title *Le fils de l'homme* (Son of Man). In the portrait, the face of the painter is obscured entirely by a green apple. For experts, the intent of the work is clear. The son of man has, forever in front of his eyes, the symbol of the fall. The apple reminds the man that the higher his ascent, the harder his fall.

47

WWW

The Jacquard weaving loom was invented in 1801 in Lyon by Joseph Marie Jacquard. He's considered to be an ancestor of the computer, on account of creating the first programmable machine. Thanks to a system of perforated cards, the loom automatically draws motifs in the weaves. To make it work, Joseph Marie draws inspiration from the work of his contemporaries.

Jean-Baptiste Falcon is the first to practice the principle of activating information-based memory using a paper ribbon. He uses the binary system. On the ribbon, there's a punched-in circle for zero (0) and a punched-in line for one (1). Basile Bouchon substitutes cardstock for paper. For his part, Jacques de Vaucanson inspires Jacquard with his cylinder of picots that allows him to bring to life his infamous automaton, the scale-sliding flute player. Jacquard's genius was to assemble these technical features to make a new machine. He created a machine with a memory, an ancestor to the computer.

At that time in Lyon, weaving is the lifeblood of a large portion of the population. Laborers who weave are called silk workers. Before Jacquard's invention, numerous people were needed to complete a job. With the perforated cards, only one or two workers were needed for the same results. They go on strike. They burn weaving looms. There's rebellion in the streets of Lyon, a silk workers' revolt. They set up barricades. Paris sends the army. It marks the beginning of the big labor movements that will greet the industrial revolution.

The Jacquard weaving loom is, in its time, a lightning strike of technological advancement. Thousands of men, women, and children risk losing their livelihoods because of its emergence, but what can be done? Ministers, councilors, committees, and bankers decide there can be no other way but forward. It's progress! The loom is exported to England. That's how an English mathematician learns about the functionality of Jacquard's machine. It gives him an idea. He'll construct a machine like the French one but, in lieu of weaving, his machine would calculate. Charles Babbage spent much of his adult life working to perfect a mechanism capable of resolving complex mathematical equations. Pascal had already invented the Pascaline, a calculating machine, in 1642. Babbage wants to build a machine capable of calculating data from outside sources, such as Jacquard's perforated cards. It's 1834, and Babbage is forty-three years old. His efforts, followed up by Ada Lovelace, give birth to the first examples of algorithmic computing.

It's not so shocking that the computer, descendent of the weaving loom, would give birth to the biggest weave in the world, the World Wide Web.

48

TWO STEVES

Despite their age difference—Steve Wozniak is twenty, Steve Jobs fifteen—their shared passion for electronics brings them together. In the fall of 1971, the two friends pull off a technical feat. Woz stumbles across the story of a certain John Draper, aka Captain Crunch, who manages to infiltrate the American telephone network thanks to a simple plastic whistle offered as a gift in a box of Cap'n Crunch cereal. Woz speaks to Jobs and they build an electronic device that replaces the whistle. It's a blue box with digital keys and a receiver that can call for free anywhere in the world. For less than a hundred dollars and a little ingenuity, two kids find themselves neck and neck with AT&T, an American telecommunications giant. "It was magic!" Jobs would say. From that moment, his belief in innovation is born. To win, you have to invent. He would also say that, without the blue box, Apple would've never seen the light of day.

Then the two Steves lose perspective. Woz tries to wrap up his studies. Jobs discovers the joys of cannabis and LSD and wants to study at Reed College in Oregon. It's one of the most reputable and expensive institutions

93

coast. His parents end up accepting his ambition. Their sacrifice will be short-lived. Arriving there at seventeen, he embraces a counter-culture lifestyle: fasting, meditation, a search for the self, Zen Buddhism, Joan Baez, Bob Dylan and acid trips. He remains enrolled for just one semester and then audits courses.

Jobs goes back to San Francisco and picks up a job as a technician for Atari. Then, like most kids his age, he decides to leave for India. By the time he returns--we're not too sure why—he has a firm conviction that Thomas Edison has achieved more advances for the human race than Karl Marx or Gandhi. Back with Atari, he reconnects with Wozniak, who's still a technician with HP. In his free time, Woz has constructed a machine that sparks Jobs's enthusiasm. In the months that follow, the Apple adventure begins to take shape. Woz is a technological genius, Jobs a genius of technological application. One without the other would amount to nothing. However, there's a worm in the apple, and the two friends quickly begin to argue. After launching the company on the stock exchange in 1980, which makes them both multi-millionaires, their views become diametrically opposed. Woz wants to enjoy life and share his profits. Jobs develops a taste for money and power, and wants to become master of the world.

On February 7, 1981, Steve Wozniak is the victim of an airplane accident that leaves him with amnesia for a while. The genius no longer has a memory. He returns to Apple for a brief period. During Wozniak's absence, Jobs has taken control of the Macintosh project, though he will soon be forced out of Apple and start his own rival company, NeXT Inc, in 1985; buy Pixar and produce Toy Story, the first feature film made entirely by computer, in 1995; and return to Apple, to save the company with the iMac and iBook, in 1997. The rest has already been overstated: the success of the iPod from 2001 on, the success of iTunes that follows, then the iPhone, and what's next?

All these successes have succeeded in erasing the fact that, had Wozniak not been there, Apple would have never existed. For the American myth of a self-made man to survive, several geniuses must be sacrificed.

49

MORTAL PROMETHEUS

In Greek mythology, Prometheus creates Man. With mud and clay, he sculpts the first humans, who come to life when graced by Athena's breath. Later, Prometheus steals the sacred fire of the gods and offers it to simple mortals. Learning this, Zeus punishes him. He ties him to a boulder and ordains an eagle to devour his liver. Each night, the organ grows back. The next day, the eagle devours it all over again. It's worth noting that this story demonstrates what we've known to be true for a very long time: a liver has the capacity to regenerate.

A bit like the Bible, where the apple is a metaphor for knowledge, the fire stolen by the Greek god represents progress and civilization. Prometheus is the father of technology. This is how we developed the habit of calling great inventors, such as De Vinci, Newton, Edison or Einstein, as the modern Prometheus. It's also the complete title of Mary Shelley's novel, *Frankenstein; or, the Modern Prometheus* (1818). There's also the case of a megalomaniac who erected a giant gold statue in the middle of an apartment complex that bears his name. That's, of course, the Prometheus at Rockefeller Center in New York, who soars over a fountain, the sacred fire in his hand. Behind him, inscribed in gold letters: "Prometheus, Teacher in Every Art, Brought the Fire That Hath Proved to Mortals a Means to Mighty Ends."

It's been said that Steve Jobs stole the idea of the mouse from Xerox, following a visit to their research laboratory, Xerox PARC (Palo Alto Research Center). Just like a modern Prometheus, he brought us the mouse and the personal computer. If we must compare him to the god of civilization, it's foremost because he also had his liver eaten, but in the 21st century, the eagle was replaced by cancer.

50

SUPER BOWL

On Sunday, January 22, 1984, millions of Americans are parked in front of their TVs. Whether alone, with family, or among friends, they're ready for a show. In a few minutes, the most anticipated sports event of the year will begin. The eighteenth edition of the Super Bowl pits the Los Angeles Raiders against the Washington Redskins. The game takes place in Tampa, Florida. Two days earlier, celebrity swimmer and actor Johnny Weissmuller dies at his Acapulco retreat.

At the end of the third quarter, the Raiders lead. The commentators reflect on the game and then announce a commercial break. Comfortably seated in their living rooms, while eating chips, drinking Budweiser and Coca-Cola, fifty million Americans find themselves faced with an apocalyptic vision. Mouths agape, they witness a cavalry of black-clad guards pursue a woman in white T-shirt and red shorts. She carries a sledgehammer. She runs toward a movie screen where a man is projected giving a speech to a crowd of ashen-faced zombies. TV viewers understand that he's Big Brother. He says, "We have created for the first time in all history a garden of pure ideology." The woman keeps running. The line of men bearing billy clubs and masks approach. Big Brother continues, "where each worker may bloom, secure from the plague of contradictory truths." The squad, the grey faces, the room. The woman begins to swivel. In a gesture worthy of an Olympic champion launching a hammer, she releases the sledgehammer into the center of the screen which explodes in a white flash of light. An off-screen voice reads aloud the following text as it appears onscreen: "On January 24th Apple Computer will introduce Macintosh. And you'll see why 1984 won't be like 1984."

So, by the time the game in Florida is back, millions of TV viewers are still in shock. They can't understand what they've just seen. The phone lines at the TV stations light up. People want to know what is a Macintosh. On the new reports that evening, reporters talk more about the success of the Apple Computer ad than they do about Los Angeles's 38-9 victory over Washington. The legend of the best ad of all time is in full swing.

Legend has it that media exposure for the ad on TV and in the press furnished Apple with millions of dollars in free advertising. As legend goes, the day Steve Jobs presents the ad to Apple's board of directors, the members are aghast. They want to block its broadcast. According to legend, this ad ushers in a new marketing strategy where flogging the merits of a product is no longer as important as telling a story. Legend confirms that by associating the computer to the liberation of the individual, Apple overcame the public's fears that computers were just a synonym for dehumanization. In reality, since the year

1984, the Super Bowl has become the most important advertising event in the United States. On the last Sunday of January, millions of Americans are in front of their TVs. In a few minutes, when the quarter ends, they'll watch the most anticipated TV ads of the year.

51

A DECK OF CARDS

This morning, Rivages finished all the work that was given him to do 'til Friday. Problem is, it's only Monday. He's sitting in front of his computer in his 13ft^2 of office space. The carpet is grey. The door is beige. The walls are white. The room is lit by two neon tubes. The desk is the shape of an L. There's a telephone, a computer, and keyboard, a lamp, and pencil holder and a note block.

To pass the time, he watches videos on YouTube. He comes across the Steve Jobs presentation of the first iPod.

They year is 2001. Steve Jobs, who was let go from Apple in 1985, was brought back in 1997. Before a room of hand-selected journalists and engineers, he explains that the computer has become the heart of a communication system that integrates video games, videos, photos, and music. Given these circumstances, Apple has decided to launch into the development of one of these sectors as a priority: music. Why music? Because the whole world loves music. Music is a universal language. It's here to stay. It's not a market that's going to disappear tomorrow. And since music is part of everyone's life, it's an enormous market, a global market. There's been the iMac and the iBook. Now there will be the iPod.

The iPod is a player for MP3 files of CD quality. It can hold a thousand songs. At the time, that's huge. For certain people, that's the equivalent of their entire music library. This new pocket-sized player boasts three big innovations:

- An ultra-flat hard drive that makes for an ultra-portable device.
- A FireWire connection that allows the transfer of a thousand songs in five minutes, all while recharging the device.
- A battery with a ten-hour capacity that can recharge in one hour.

To top off the spectacle, the device is the size of a deck of cards! The iPod appears on the screen. Jobs says, "And here's one right here in my pocket." He shows it to the public who, impressed, applaud with enthusiasm.

Rivages is also impressed. He's never seen a marketing presentation so well realized. And he's seen a lot of them. This one is simple and clear. It gets straight to the point, but most of all it recounts a story. It recounts the birth of a product. We get the feeling of being there at its delivery. With an ingenious slogan, a thousand songs in your pocket, a strong image, a deck of cards, Jobs touches upon all the quintessential features of a product launch. That's its force: get to the essential, magnify the simplicity. Rivages thinks to himself that, if his marketing colleagues could even aspire to the heights of Jobs's ankle, even that would be enormous progress. He closes the video and taps into Google: employment opportunities.

52

AD INFINITUM

When he begins to count, my son often asks me how high numbers go. I tell him that there is no end, that we can always count higher. It takes him some time to accept the idea of infinity. Later, I explain to him that, if we use the decimal system, it's because our ancestors, like us, began by counting on their fingers and they had but ten.

Other calculating systems have been invented, with five symbols, eight symbols, or only two symbols, as in computing. You can write all the numbers in the world with only two symbols. For example, I can write 1984 with 0's and 1's, like this: 11111000000. It's longer than in a ten-symbol system, but it expresses the same number. It's known as the binary system; without it, the computer would not exist. In everyday life, we use another very practical system. That system is the alphabet. Without it, the word 'computer' would not exist. With twenty-six symbols, we can express ourselves ad infinitum.

53

THE DEMO

There's a colloquium of computer experts. A black-and-white poster announces the conference, Monday afternoon at San Francisco's Congress Center. In the top-left corner, a photo of a man, hair slicked back, white shirt, black tie and blazer to match. The man stares out into the future. It's Douglas Carl Engelbart. He's an engineer and director at Stanford's Research Institute in Menlo Park, California: A research center dedicated to the development of human intelligence. Dr. Engelbart will deliver a ninety-minute lecture in the main amphitheater.

At the same time, the Diggers, a mime troupe led by Peter Coyote, are performing at a park in the city. The event is kept secret until the last moment, since the actors don't have the necessary permits. The anarchist hippie mime artists are not ones for asking permission. Barely has the performance gotten underway when armed police officers come to round up the members of the troupe and their few spectators. "Gather 'em up in the truck, damn gang of hippies. Why don't you cut your hair, you flea-infested dirt bags, instead of dancing in the streets. For fuck's sake." To announce their performances and print their newspaper, the Diggers set up The Communication

Company, the propaganda arm of the organization. In the first edition of the Company, Richard Brautigan publishes his famous poem, "All Watched Over by Machines of Loving Grace". Cybernetics is its main theme. As Peter Coyote negotiates with the police chief, Doug Engelbart commits a slip of the tongue in the opening moments of his lecture. Instead of saying that computers are "instantly responsive", he says they're "instantly responsible". A machine that will be responsible, is that what we're really dreaming up? You have to go see the latest Kubrick, 2001, Space Odyssey, to learn about the intelligent computer HAL 9000 (if you take the letters that come right after the H, A and L, you get IBM). Engelbart's lecture was subtitled The Demo and it can be found online at this address: https://web.stanford.edu/dept/SUL/library/extra4/sloan/MouseSite/1968Demo.html.

On that day—December 9, 1968—at 3:45pm, in the San Francisco Congress Center's amphitheater, Doug Engelbart presents the results from six years of research at his laboratory, the Stanford Research Institute. It constitutes the first videoconference in the history of humanity. Over the course of ninety minutes, Engelbart presents for the first time, to a public of a thousand engineers, the use of a mouse and a text editor that allows for the copying and pasting of information, the ability to select with a pointer, to move, to edit, and to share in a modern telecommunication network. For ninety minutes, hundreds of people witness the birth of the computer as we know it today. Engelbart is one of the fathers of modern computing.

Members of Engelbart's team will eventually leave for Xerox PARC (Palo Alto Research Center) and continue to develop the mouse, as well as other interfaces and protocols that set the network in motion. That's how Steve Jobs will discover these new technological advances. They will form the key to his future success: the Macintosh. His epiphany is Doug Engelbart's brainchild. The politics of the Communication Company was, "Love is communication".

54

GRAN HERMANO

We had just crossed Spain in a Peugeot 206, the windows down, at forty degrees in the sun. Our eyes burned with the redness of scorched earth, the greyness of abandoned stones, the greenness of irrigated fields, the yellowness of withered crops. Our thoughts were among the plains and the mountains, the farm villages where we stopped to allow a herd of sheep to pass, the bell towers lost in the distance, down there to the left. And also the ochre bricks, the hanging hams, several flashes of ceramic, azulejos.

At the end of this route, we drove up to the top, to the summit where we viewed the white village and the blue dome. We checked into a room. We claimed the key. We brought up our bags, some beers, olives, red wine. On the terrace we put our feet up on the table. In tandem, we looked out to the sea.

The Spanish translate "Big Brother" as "Gran Hermano". Why do we, in French, use the English term? Why don't we translate it as "Grand Frère", like the Spanish? It's a question. We tackle it with red wine. I eat another olive. Down with Big Brother! À bas Big Brother! ¡Abajo el Gran Hermano!

55

PSEUDONYM

In the Year of our Lord 1600, in London, powerful merchants form the British East India Company. With the benediction of the queen, Elizabeth I, they're going to spread their commerce all the way to Asia. They prepare grand expeditions. They recruit the best captains. They engage the most able sailors. They take tons of supplies on board. They release the mooring lines. They cross the Cape of Good Hope. They dock. They build cabins. They install a trading post. They negotiate with people who venerate many-armed gods and elephant-headed gods.

Not all the ships return. The losses are sometimes heavy, but the profits that eclipse them are enormous. Tea, saltpeter, silk, and indigo that overflow from the holds bring in fortunes for the merchants. For every investment of one-thousand sterling, they reap three thousand. So they plunge deeper into adventure, in more expeditions. It's only the beginning.

Over time, the Company can raise armies and take power wherever it chooses. They put to shame the Portuguese, Dutch, and French. They silence those who speak of the land of their ancestors. With weapons or money, they break revolts. India remains British until 1947.

In 1903, Richard is an English subject from a good family. Like many of his compatriots, he's a functionary in the colonial bureaucracy. He works in the office in charge of the opium trade. It's an excessively lucrative trade. The drive to keep selling this drug in China would lead to the Chinese War fifty years later, and to the annexation of Hong Kong afterward. For Richard, it's good work. He does miss the climate of his native England. India's heat and monsoons tire him to no end. It's nothing compared to what his wife, Ida, endures for nine months. She's due any day now, in Motihari. It's a boy. One year later, Ida can no longer take India and returns home with their children.

Life is easier in Oxfordshire. The son goes to good schools. They play bridge and cricket. The years pass and the boy becomes, in turn, an honorable subject of Her Majesty. At the age of twenty, a taste for adventure wins him over. He decides to take up travel to Asia again. He enlists in the British imperial police in Burma. That's how Eric Arthur Blair enters the world. The next major event of his life will be that of George Orwell, his pseudonym.

56

ALL LIGHTS OFF

One day, we were sixteen years old, and we had our driving licenses. Returning from a baseball game, on the highway, we came up with the idea to try out some stunts. We began by driving with all our lights off. With the two cars speeding side by side, we got the idea to climb out of one and into the other. We were going more than one hundred and twenty kilometers per hour.

It's the first thing that Rivages thinks about when his son enters the world. Maybe one day he'll hold on for balance between two cars driving along at more than one hundred kilometers per hour on a highway, with all the lights off. To not see this he closes his eyes.

57

ENIGMA

He has a routine in a mostly empty bar. He sits in front
of the barman and orders a scotch. He hasn't yet begun
to drink it and he's already not alone. A young marine
on leave orders the same thing. When their glasses are
empty they both leave, one after the next.

He goes to church every Sunday. He believes it can
protect him. At this time in England, sodomy is a crime.
Like Oscar Wilde before him, he risks the worst. The trial
gets a lot of attention. He's an eminent scientist. To avoid
prison, they offer him a plea bargain of chemical castra-
tion. Alan Turing accepts. A hell awaits him. There's no
way out other than suicide.

During the Second World War, German submarines,
the U-boats, circle England. At the bottom of the sea
they're blind. They must communicate with radar stations
on land to sink the ships of the English, Americans, Canadians, etc. The Allies intercept the messages but they're
coded. To decipher them, they must find the key to the
code used—the Enigma code. English mathematicians
work day and night to find the answer. To get there,
they begin constructing electronic machines capable of

producing, in a few minutes, calculations that a human being would take days to work through. This is where the Second World War gives birth to the first computers, like the Robinson and the Colossus in England, the Mark 1 by IBM in the United States, and the Z3 in Germany. It's the kind of machine that can execute several additions per second, more than ten multiplications per minute, and weighs between one and five tons. Alan Turing is recognized as the man who broke the Enigma code. He made a significant contribution to the victory of the Allies against the Axis of Evil.

After the war, Turing pursues his work and conceives of an imaginary machine. It's a machine of disconcerting simplicity that, in its ability to realize a gigantic number of operations in a few seconds, is more powerful than all complex machines. With the machine that bears his name, Turing puts to paper the fundamentals of what will become the modern computer.

Turing also bequeathed his name to a test that aimed to bridge the gap between human being and machine as its goal. Could machines be made to think? The Turing test takes place every year. A man and a computer each converse with judges for five minutes. If the computer tricks more than thirty percent of the judges, it wins. It's yet to happen. Turing's theoretical postulations led to a number of speculations and fictions. Ridley Scott's film Blade Runner, is one of the most well-known manifestations of Turing's ideas. The cyborgs are his children. In 1950 Turing wrote, "I think that by the end of the century, the use of words and common opinions by educated people will have changed so much that we can talk about machines that think without the fear of being contradicted."

Turing saved the lives of thousands of soldiers. He raised essential philosophical questions. His homosexuality became his cross to bear. The chemical treatment he underwent to extinguish his desire for men plunged him into deep depression. A fervent admirer of *Snow White*, he puts an end to his days on June 7, 1954 by eating an apple laced with cyanide. For a long time it's been said that the Apple logo, an apple with a bite taken out, was a subtle tribute to Alan Turing, one of the fathers of modern computing. The real reason is that the best logo for a company that calls itself Apple is an apple. There's no need to be a super-computer capable of decrypting the Enigma code to get that.

58

CLEAR THE MIND

In the seventeenth century, Leibniz studies papers related to Fou-hi to develop his own philosophy and logic system. From fullness to emptiness, we pass along algebraic calculations to the machine. Leibniz also improves upon the Pascaline, the calculating machine invented by Blaise Pascal in 1642. They were aided in their enterprise by logarithms that are credited to John Napier.

For a long time, Rivages continues to follow the course of events that lead to the development of the com-puter. He rediscovers Aristotle and the fundamentals of his logic: a proposition can be true or false, but cannot be true and false. In the fifth century BC, in the Middle East, Rivages comes across the first calculating tools, the counting frame and the abacus. He travels between Bombay and Baghdad, where the invention of zero is equally crucial.

But all that is nothing compared to the scientific and technical advances that were produced in the hundred years since the middle of the nineteenth century. Taken by the whirlwind that sweeps him up, Rivages returns to Fou-hi and, sitting at his desk, he attempts to clear his mind.

59

ON STANDBY

At the end of class, the biology teacher asks Gabriel if he can come babysit his two children tomorrow evening. In 1984, Gabriel is fifteen years old. Faced with the possibility of making a little pocket money, he says yes. That's how he finds himself standing in the middle of the living room before two kids who are seven and nine years old, and just as intimidated as he is. The parents explain pajama time, how the kids brush their teeth, their ten minutes of reading, the night light in the corridor. We won't be back late, they say. The TV turns on like this, and the kids know how to work the computer.

They get to know each other. The play Lego and a bit of hide and seek. They laugh a lot and the kids show Gabriel the new Macintosh computer that their parents just bought. At seven and nine years old, they explain how it starts up, where to put the diskette, where to click, and how to play Pinball Quest. There are also many other diskettes with many other games: *Dark Castle*, Breakout, *Tetris*, *Asteroids*, *Snake*, *Airborne*, *MacAttack*, *Choplifter*, *Robotron: 2084*, *Pacman* and *Apple Panic*.

From that evening on, every time his biology teacher asks him to watch his kids, Gabriel says yes. Ever since his first visit, he's on standby for those kids, and the Macintosh is on standby for him.

60

MEMEX

Vannevar Bush competes his studies at MIT then works for the US Army. During the Second World War he's in charge of recruiting team members for the Manhattan Project. There's a little bit of him in the first atomic bomb. As Director of Research at the Pentagon, he publishes an article in 1945 entitled "As We May Think". In it, he describes a machine called the Memex. He imagines a machine that permits people to stock all their books, all their archives, all their mail, etc. This same machine will be capable of accessing all these documents in an efficient and rapid manner. For Vannevar Bush, this machine will become a surplus of memory for its user.

Doug Engelbart is twenty years old when he reads this article. An electrical engineer, he grew up in Oregon. During the war, he works on radars. Fascinated by the idea of Memex, he enrolls at Berkeley to study the budding science of computing. A doctorate in his pocket, he contacts General Electric and Hewlett-Packard in the hope of developing a machine inspired by Memex, a machine that can make humans more intelligent. The industrials aren't interested. Dejected, he applies at

Stanford University for a professorship. They write him back stating that no such discipline yet exists for computers at Stanford. They inform him that, nevertheless, right next door to the campus, the US Army funds a multi-disciplinary research laboratory, the Stanford Research Institute. The Institute works on artificial intelligence and data storage. Engelbart is hired. It's the beginning of the sixties, and he can't yet know that he'll be among those who'll invent the personal computer, the mouse, the copy-paste and the Internet.

Tomahawk cruise missiles became famous in 1991 during the Gulf War. Their production is credited to Raytheon, a company founded by Vannevar Bush and two of his colleagues in 1922. They can also be credited with the invention of microwaves. According to the company's website, Raytheon means "the light of gods". From Hiroshima to Baghdad, one must always be suspicious of gods.

61

PONG

In 1972, *Pong* is Atari's first video game to hit the market. Rivages played it for the first time when he was ten years old with his cousin Luc. Each player turned a button that moved a rectangle up and down to ricochet a ball. If a ball slipped past, the opponent scored a point. It was disconcertingly simple. The immense success of Pong launched the video game industry.

Later on, Atari put out another game that everyone knows. Its principle is similar to that of *Pong*. At the top of the screen, there's a wall of bricks. At the bottom of the screen, there's a cursor. You have to move the cursor to ricochet a ball back to the bricks. The tapped bricks disappear. The game is called *Breakout*, which in French may have been translated as *Casse-briques*. He no longer remembers. On the other hand, he does know that Nolan Bushnell, Atari's boss, asks Steve Jobs to work on the electronic circuit board for the game. He offers him a bonus for the simplifications he makes to the circuit board. Jobs gives the task to his friend Steve Wozniak, who works at Hewlett-Packard. Bushnell is astonished at the results. He believes Jobs did the work. Jobs collects the bonus of a thousand dollars and gives two hundred to Wozniak, telling him it's half the total. At least there's no way to cheat when playing *Pong*.

62

CLARA HAGOPIAN

In a few days, it's his birthday. He'll be seven years old. But today is Sunday. It's raining. His father is in the garage, his mother in the kitchen. Stretched out in front of the TV he watches an old Tarzan movie. Jane explains that she must go back to her father: "Those are tears, Tarzan. You've never seen tears before, have you? You know why they're there? To say goodbye. I must go with him. (*Tears.*) Oh yes, I must. I can't do it. He loves me."

Tarzan: "Love?"

Jane: "He loves me too. I'm all he's got. Goodbye."

Tarzan: "Goodbye?"

Jane: "Yes. Oh Tarzan… Tarzan, don't look at me, not like that. If you do, I can't be able to go, and I must. Do you see? Goodbye, my dear."

He's seven years old. This scene bores him. He could turn off the TV, but it's Sunday and it's raining. His body weighs tons. His head feels like it's in a viciously thick fog. He has no ambition. A break for ads wakes him up a little. Mister Ed, the talking horse, talks up the latest Studebaker Lark. Mister Ed, the talking horse, can always make him laugh.

After the break, Jane, her father and all the members of the expedition are captured by the mean Pygmies. Back in the village, the sacrifice begins. Bound at the neck with a vine, the prisoners are thrown one by one into a hole. It's the lair of the beast. At the bottom of the pit is a giant, monstrous gorilla that slaughters its victims one after the other. At the moment that Jane falls at the feet of the monster, Tarzan suddenly appears in the middle of the carnage, his knife in hand. The ape-man lets loose his cry. A horde of elephants appears. They destroy the village and crush all the Pygmies in their path. Tarzan kills the monster, saves Jane, but can't do anything for the father of his love. James Parker dies in an elephant cemetery.

That night, little Steve Jobs has an awful nightmare. His father is devoured by a monster who resembles the gorilla. The rain has stopped. He howls. He cries, "Mooooooooom! Daaaaaaad!" His mother turns on the light in the hall. She sits down next to him. She takes him in her arms. She comforts him. She asks him to recount the bad dream to chase it away. She goes to get him a glass of apple juice. She's back. All is well. He's reassured. He must sleep now. He has school tomorrow. He falls back asleep. What can it change that Clara Hagopian is his adoptive mother and not his biological mother?

63

AND THE MONA LISA SMILES

At the Louvre, my son had but one goal, to see the Mona Lisa. After waiting in many lineswe located Room 6 in the Denon wing. There she was. Yes, there were a lot of people. Yes, the canvas is protected behind reinforced glass. Yes, all the visitors take photos. Yes, I had to pick my son up in my arms so he could get a better look. Yes, the canvas is not that big. Yes, my son was a bit disappointed. Yes, it's probably the most renowned painting in the world. No, people don't go to see the *Mona Lisa* to see Leonardo Da Vinci's art. Yes, people go see *La Gioconda* to say they've seen *La Gioconda*. King Francis I acquired the work in 1518. The complete title is *Portrait of Lisa Gherardini, Wife of Francesco del Giocondo*. On the wall facing her, an impressive painting—*The Wedding Feast at Cana*, by Veronese. It's the biggest one in the museum. It measures ten meters wide by six meters and sixty-six centimeters high.

As for me, what I absolutely wanted to see was the Louvre's only Bruegel. So we kept moving along through the rooms and halls. We walked for a long time. We arrived in the Schools of the North section of the

Richelieu wing, on the second floor. We asked a security guard where we could find Bruegel. Hidden at the back of a room, in an alcove, we found it. The painting is small. It's three centimeters smaller than an iPad. It's called *The Beggars*. In it, one sees five deformed cripples. They are all on crutches. Three of them have no legs. They present an adequately apocalyptic vision. My son didn't like it. I think that the three legless beggars in the painting suffer from ergotism.

Ergotism seriously ravaged Europe in the Middle Ages. It was contracted mostly from eating bread contaminated with Claviceps purpurea. It's a fungus that develops on grains of rye. It grows by taking the shape of an ergot, a rooster's spur. That's why in French it's called the ergot de seigle—a rye grain's spur that causes Claviceps purpurea. People get sick by eating bread made with flour that's contaminated with the fungus. Symptoms are wide-ranging. If you're lucky, you get away with only diarrhea, vomiting, and hallucinations. You can also have convulsions. With a little less luck, you get gangrene. *Claviceps purpurea* is a vasoconstrictor; it reduces the circulation of blood. If you keep eating contaminated bread, blood will cease to circulate to the tips of your fingers and the lobes of your ears. Slowly but surely, you'll begin to fall to bits.

Bruegel the Elder paints *The Beggars* in 1568. We have to wait until the Age of Enlightenment for doctors and botanists to understand that *Claviceps purpurea* is what contaminates bread and that the bread then contaminates people. We have to wait even longer for the spur's powder, ergotin, to be used to stop hemorrhaging. As we can read in the *Larousse universel: dictionnaire encyclopédique de 1922*, this remedy should be prescribed "to treat hemorrhaging only when the infant has been completely cleared from its womb, including all placental debris that can remain after the delivery".

During the Second World War, a Swiss chemist worked on the rye fungus. A medication to counter hemorrhaging had already been devised. Could there be other applications? One evening in April 1943, like all other evenings, the chemist returned home by bicycle. He works at the Sandoz laboratory in Basel. In Poland, fifty thousand Jews in the Warsaw ghetto take up arms. They're going to fight being deported to the camps. They will all be massacred within a month.

The chemist is heading back home on his bicycle when all of a sudden the road begins to move beneath his tires. He goes flying, leaping up in the air. The fronts of houses ripple. Arriving home, he gets himself to bed. Floating before his eyes is an incessant kaleidoscope of vibrant colors. His head turns, he feels like laughing, crying, he stays paralyzed in his bed. Then, softly, after several hours, everything returns to normal. Albert Hofmann has just lived through the first acid trip in modern history. By accident, he'd absorbed lysergic acid diethylamide, which is derived from rye spurs. In English, it's better known as LSD.

Thinking today of the numerous visions of saints, like the resurrection of Christ as seen by Teresa of Ávila, those could have been caused as a reaction to the rye spurs. Just thinking of all the testaments to visions of Hell and sightings of the Virgin over the course of centuries, they could've maybe been the result of contaminated bread. Some of the most highly regarded works in the world could've been produced under the influence of this drug. We've always believed that intoxicated people were possessed by the devil. The trials of witches in Salem could've been the impressionable results of ergotism. In those days, when someone started vomiting all over the place, started rolling on the ground in their own feces, howling and screaming, people thought he was possessed and tied him to the stake.

LSD was first declared illegal in California in 1966 by the state's governor, Ronald Reagan. Today, if you want to know what an acid trip is like by legal means, you can watch *2001: A Space Odyssey*. The final stretch, "Jupiter and Beyond the Infinite", the voyage scene is considered a classic. Otherwise, there's *Easy Rider* and the cemetery scene toward the end. As for me, headphones on my ears, what I prefer is launching my sixties playlist in iTunes and activating the visual effects (option "View Visualizer" from the "View" menu). Steve Jobs himself once said that the feature reminded him of the acid trips of his youth. He also said that, if you've never experienced LSD at least once in your life, then you've missed something.

In Hieronymus Bosch paintings, I see him eat rye bread, and the Mona Lisa smiles.

64

AND YOUR SISTER?

One day, Steve Jobs said that his biological parents were nothing more than a reservoir of spermatozoids and eggs. He said that his real parents were the ones who raised him, his adoptive parents. He can't really be faulted for thinking that. Later on, Jobs found his biological mother and learned that he had a sister, Mona. He said that, at their first meeting, he immediately felt close to her. He felt connected to his sister. With Mona, Jobs had the impression of rediscovering a family.

As for me, I say you should make up your mind, Steve! Either you care about genealogy and all family members are part of it, or you don't care and your sister is no more yours than mine!

65

VIVRE LE QUÉBEC LIBRE

The story is well known. In 1983, Jobs convinced the president of Pepsi-Cola, John Sculley, to quit by asking him if he preferred to continue selling sugar water for the rest of his life or join Apple instead and change the world.

Sculley begins making his name in 1975. He is then director of marketing at Pepsi. His mission is to win portions of the market from Coca-Cola. To do so, he launches a unique campaign that was called the Pepsi Challenge. It consists of blind taste tests that make for great television advertising. It works out really well, and Sculley rises through the ranks.

In 1976, there was a Pepsi ad with René Simard for the Quebec Carnival: "Rise up to the Pepsi Challenge, let yourself be swept away by the taste!" Next there were those with Claude Meunier dressed up as a hockey player speaking to Lionel Duval, host of *La soirée du hockey*. Quebec is the only region in the world where sales of Pepsi surpass those of Coca-Cola. As De Gaulle said, "Vivre le Québec libre!"

66

METEOR

One of my most cherished childhood memories is the summer when, with my cousin Luc, we took my grandmother's car apart piece by piece and screw by screw. It was a magnificent black Mercury Meteor from the seventies with rear headlights in the shape of red arrows. It truly looked like a meteorite crossing space. It was a shooting star. The upholstery was red faux-leather.

We must've been around eight and twelve years old. The black Meteor had finally died after years of good and loyal service. My grandmother door-to-door deliveries and sometimes she used the car as a taxi. All she needed was for passengers to pay for the gas and they'd be off discovering the world. That gave her a life beyond the farm and church on Sundays. This is how she visited Manic 5, Abitibi, Toronto, Boston, and the Gaspésie.

As far back as I can remember, I've always liked taking apart anything that could be unassembled. Telephones, radios, alarm clocks, watches, old toys and toasters. I also took apart two or three TV sets. So that summer was something of a pinnacle when my grandmother let us take her car apart. It was like making it to the finals of the Olympic Games. We played at being mechanics for days and days.

When you take apart something mechanical, even if you're not aware of all the subtleties, you get to a point where you broadly understand how it works. With electronics, it's different. There are thousands of components and circuits that can't be opened. The mechanism is invisible. It's like batteries. I've often opened them up with the smack of a hammer. Inside, there's nothing but metal rods, cardboard, and a liquid that's a bit slimy. If you don't understand the principle of chemical reaction that produces electricity, there's nothing to glean from opening one up.

For this reason, at twenty years old I enrolled in electrical engineering at university. I wanted to understand how a computer, a microwave, an electronic circuit function. After two months of studies, I understood. It's a matter of switches based in Boolean logic. It all relies on components that can do only one thing: allow electricity to pass or don't allow electricity to pass, depending on the voltage. It's as simple as that. Like a microscopic switch. The best material to make the switches is silicon, an element that's abundantly available on Earth. There's a lot of it in sand.

When the current is not allowed to pass, it's a zero; when the current passes through, it's a one. That's how a computer counts. And if it counts fast enough and efficiently enough, it's because of the little circuits that allow or don't allow for the passage of its current. A computer contains millions of circuits on a surface the size of a microchip. I confess that the explanation sounds trivial, but when I understood that, I dropped out of my studies in electrical engineering. The mystery had been solved, and I could move on to something else.

In the end, when we were done taking it all apart, there was nothing left but the sheet-metal carcass of my grandmother's Meteor. It was like a giant black whale had beached itself behind the house. My cousin and I were two glorious harpooners coming back to port, our desire sated. Then, in the background, we heard my grandmother cry out, "Time for dinner, boys!"

67

SHEEP 3

Yesterday, my son couldn't mouth the word "papa". This morning he says, "Papa, pass me the cereal box please." Yesterday, he couldn't hold a pencil between his fingers. This morning he draws blue waves on a white sheet of paper. We'd gone to the beach this past Saturday. Yesterday, he bleated, "Sheep, Sheep, Sheep" so we'd give him his stuffed sheep. Today, he talks to it, saying, "Look, Sheep, nice book! Sit down, Sheep! Be quiet, Sheep! Sheep is happy." Yesterday, he was still in his mother's belly, and today he has his own. Every time I look at him, I get tickles in mine.

68

A TURING MACHINE

"A Turing machine is determinist if, for each state p and each symbol a, there exists as well a transition of the form p, a → q, b, x. When the machine is determinist, the ensemble E of transitions is also called the function of transition and is noted as δ. The function δ associated to each pair (p, a) the unique triplet (q, b, x), if it exists, so that p, a → q, b, x, x becomes a transition."

I can't bring myself around to the belief that this means anything to anyone.

69

LAND AND FREEDOM

This all happened in an art-house cinema in Toronto. We went to see Ken Loach's *Land and Freedom*. A film that's not easy to follow if you're not already familiar with the history of the Spanish Civil War. There's the communists, the anarchists, the Republicans, Franco, etc. It's filled with betrayals. Hitler's advancing in Germany. With Mussolini, fascism has triumphed in Italy.

The Spanish Civil War pits the Republicans to the left against the Nationalists to the right. The communists, the anarchists, the socialists and the international brigades fight against Franco's army, who defend the wealthy land and property owners, the king, and the church. The problem for the republicans, on top of lacking means and arms, are their internal conflicts. At a certain point in the film, you lose track of how the Workers Party of Marxist Unification (POUM) and the National Confederation of Labor (CNT) have been entangled.

During Ken Loach's *Land and Freedom*, in an art-house cinema in Toronto, I put my hand on her thigh. At the moment where Robert Capa captured the mythic image of a Republican who, shot in the chest, opens his arms in a cross before falling to the ground, she set her hand on mine.

George Orwell, Ernest Hemingway and André Malraux all fought in Spain as part of the International Brigades. They wanted to preserve an idea of freedom vomited out by the Francoists, the fascists, and Nazis. It was a pretty heroic gesture. Later on, when George Orwell's wife, Eileen O'Shaughnessy, was unable to get pregnant, the couple decided to adopt a boy. To erase all traces of the biological parents, Orwell burned the child's birth records. That was a pretty mean thing to do. In a photo from his youth, George Orwell, whose real name is Eric Blair, has a moustache, the same one worn by Hitler and Charlie Chaplin. Certain contradictions engender major works. In 1984, the party doctrine is summed up in these words:

WAR IS PEACE
FREEDOM IS SLAVERY
IGNORANCE IS STRENGTH

That evening, as we left the art-house cinema in Toronto, we kissed. Ten years later, my son is unaware that there's a little bit of *Land and Freedom* in him.

70

SURPRISE

I took off on my own for one week and headed to the coast to write. I write for eight hours, from morning till midnight. At 7pm, I take a break. I go for a swim. I head to the beach. I get down to the sand via an access ramp. There aren't many of us here. No one is in the water. I slip on my bathing trunks. I do a few lengths, even though I have none of the skills of a Weissmuller. Getting out, I go to rinse off at the shower near the access ramp. That's where I spot a fallen sign in the sand. I read what's written on it: Swimming temporarily not allowed. Toxic danger!"

71

MOBY DICK AND THE SIRENS

We all have our own white whale. We endeavor to reach a
goal, to understand something, but it escapes us. We feel
that, if one day we do get there, it could hurt. Be we make a
go of it anyways. It's stronger than us. We have to seize the
moment, take the giant leap. We must plunge into, take off
with the adventure. There's something out there that we
must claim. In *Moby Dick*, Captain Ahab tracks the white
whale. When he was younger, the whale had cost him his
leg. Ahab is obsessed. He needs revenge. He wants to pay
back the whale for his wooden leg. In fact it's a sperm
whale, which is why it's referred to as a white whale. We all
have our own white whale. We don't all clamor for revenge
from it, though. We'd like to understand it better. We'd
like to know why we have to chase after it. We'd prefer to
remain at port. We could choose to watch our kids grow
up in peace, smoke a pipe, nothing more. But the song of
the whales and those of sirens tug at us. Only Ulysses had
the strength to survive their call by covering his ears and
tying himself to the mast of his ship. The common man
succumbs.

72

AIR-CONDITIONED MOTOR HOME

The most incredible part of the story in which Steve Jobs is kicked out of his own company in 1985 is not that we revisit it to hunt for his shortcomings, but to view it as a traumatic event. It becomes a foundational element of his myth, the proof that warrants his status as hero. We're almost brought to tears. That's what's incredible. The story is so well told that we want to cry over the tragic destiny of a wounded man. Poor Stevie, he has no more work. He's humiliated. We treated him like a dog.

I'm trying to tell you something. In 1985, Steve Jobs is thirty years old and has one hundred million dollars in the bank. If I'd gone through the same thing, I wouldn't have been very traumatized at all. Much worse can happen to a person in life. It's a desert crossing maybe, but with a fridge full of beer in an air-conditioned motor home.

73

MAYBE NOT

It resembled a Monopoly box but heavier. I set down the package. I ripped away the giftwrap. I was still a child. I'd always loved playing with batteries, light bulbs, and little electric motors that I'd remove from broken toys. So, for this birthday, I'd received a kit of 101 electronic projects. It consisted of a wooden tray with resistors, transistors, a control button, a photo-electric cell, a VU-meter, an amplifier, condensers, a red light, etc. They were all connected to little numbered coils. All you had to do was take the precut electric wires and connect them across the board. There was a color for each length of wire: reds, yellows, blues, whites, blacks.

The experiments were more or less complex. The first one I did, I believe, was the siren. You simply follow the instructions and be patient: connect coils 12 and 26 with a red wire; connect coils 17 and 31 with a black wire; connect coils 20 and 22 with a yellow wire; connect coils 22 and 31 with a blue wire, and so on. At the end, I'd pressed on the button and the sound of a siren rang out. Wrrrrrrrrrrrrrrrr!

After, I put together the darkness sensor. When blacked out, its red light lit up. I tried the radio. It didn't work. The lie detector also didn't come together as planned. However, I really enjoyed the telegraph and its Morse code. When I'd just turned ten, I pretended I was Thomas Edison or Graham Bell. But then I got bored.

It appears that, at age ten, Steve Jobs had received a kit that let him assemble a radio receiver himself. It appears he was also able to listen to Elvis and Dylan sing on the machine that he'd built. Maybe if I'd been in Silicon Valley in the mid-50s, I could have had more success with electronics? Maybe I could've invented the personal computer? Maybe not.

74

ACCORDING TO ARAGON

For a long time, he'd believed that reality would suffice. He had, for a long time, believed that the facts spoke for themselves. If you make the effort, you end up understanding. You search, you inform yourself, you document. You make connections and you draw conclusions. It's pretty much scientific. For this reason, he loves science and biographies, because they rely on the facts. They're supported by something solid. There's no question here of fables and magic, of the Loch Ness monster or Santa Claus, of telluric forces or the transmigration of souls. No, to make sense of living, you need the lucidity of facts. You reconstruct the story and mock the ignoramuses. You make fun of the easily dazzled who've understood nothing of the myth of Plato's cave. Hey there! All of it's nothing but an illusion! Stop fighting over borders. Stop sacrificing yourself for a religion. You're being manipulated.

Then, one day, you realize that you've made a mistake. Alone against everything, you've done wrong. It's not facts that give meaning to life, it's the account of the facts, the way in which they're recounted. But "by the time one learns to live, it's already too late". According to Aragon.

75

OH MY GOD!

Bertrand Russell receives the Kalinga Prize for the popularization of science in 1957. In the speech he delivers for this occasion, he regrets the growing divide between literary culture and scientific culture. He calls for the teaching of scientific history at schools. If Homer, Shakespeare, and Beethoven hadn't existed, our daily lives wouldn't have been that affected. However, if Pythagoras, Galileo, Watt and Einstein hadn't existed, life would be profoundly different. Russell ends with the words: "The modern theory and practice of nuclear physicists has made evident with dramatic suddenness that complete ignorance of the world of science is no longer compatible with survival."

Steve Jobs liked to take himself for a Leonardo da Vinci. He saw in the Italian the perfect figure of a renaissance man, at once artistic and scientific, poet and technician. For him, the portraitist of the Mona Lisa represents the epitome of collaboration between art and science. All his life, Jobs aimed for this duality. He wants to marry the most perfect technology with the most refined design. It's no accident that da Vinci's words appear at the header of the promotional brochure for the Apple II in 1977: "Simplification is the ultimate sophistication." It sounds even better in Italian: "La simplicità è l'ultima sofisticazione." Over time, the maxim is even attributed to Jobs himself. Question: to whom do these citations belong?

- Be the change that you want to see in the world.
- Choose a job you love and you'll never have to work a day in your life.
- When words lose their meaning, people lose their freedom.
- The whole is larger than the sum of its parts.
- Forgive us our sins, for we also forgive everyone who sins against us.
- Remember that your son is not your son, but the son of his times.
- You won't find what you're looking for unless you look within.
- You can only become what you want to be by staying true to who you are.
- Everything that develops toward its extreme will also produce its opposite.

Bertrand Russell, born in Wales in 1872, is one of the most renowned philosophers of the twentieth century. To his English contemporaries who exclaimed "Oh my God!", he systematically replied, "He doesn't exist!"

76

I CHING

We met when I asked her for a match during the course's break. We were in the same Sociology of Literature lecture. One December evening when it was too cold, we went to grab a beer at Dogue, on St. Denis Street. After last call, I crashed at her place.

That's how I came to know the *I Ching: The Book of Changes*. It was a fat yellow book on the coffee table in her living room. You had to play heads or tails with three coins. We did that six times in a row. It resulted in either an even or uneven total that we noted with a solid line or a broken line, the yin or the yang. There were sixty-four possible outcomes ($26 = 64$). We then read the numbered texts that corresponded to the result.

It's sometimes said that the I Ching and its sixty-four hexagrams, based on only two symbols, the yin and the yang, are the first binary representation in the world. Wise Chinese such as Confucius had explained the world from the basis of the original polarity.

To pass the time, she pulled out the I Ching for me. Afterward, we made love on the living room carpet. It was much later on, a little before we broke up, that I tried it again in secret. I know what you're thinking, a book of divination, but you mustn't take me for an eccentric. But that evening, I truly touched the depths. And, it's well known, divinations, gods, religions, they all come down to that. They seek to connect you to something even if it's completely false. We're in the mode of full-on fiction, but it makes us feel good. So I tossed three pennies six times and I went to see which hexagram my result corresponded to:

> The noble man puts his person to rest before he moves. He contemplates in his soul before speaking. He affirms his relations before asking for something. Having put these three things in order, he is perfectly secure. If not, those who want to harm him come near.

It seemed pretty complicated to me. It was much simpler to toss a coin for a heads or tails. The coin landed with its tail facing up, and that evening at dinner I told her that we were breaking up. From her side, she didn't need the I Ching to decide that I was a jackass.

77

SAINT GABRIEL BRINGS GOOD NEWS

In the Bible, Gabriel announces to Zachariah that his wife Elizabeth will have a son. He will become Saint John the Baptist. Gabriel is also the one who announces to Mary that, despite her virginity, she's pregnant with the Son of God. In Islam, he is known by the Arab name of Djibril. He's the one who reveals the verses of the Koran to Muhammad.

On January 12, 1951, by papal brief, Pope Pius XII proclaimed Gabriel "the celestial patron of all activities relative to telecommunications and all their technicians and laborers". Which makes him the patron saint of the Internet. The proverb that accompanies it is Saint Gabriel brings good news. Not sure that the Virgin Saint would be fully in agreement with that.

78

A BICYCLE FOR OUR MINDS

It's a story he's written several times before. It shines a little more every time he tells it. At the beginning, it's still fastidious. He speaks of an article that he just happened to read in *Scientific American* when was about twelve years old. At length, he explains the research conducted by the scientists on the relationship between the distance travelled by an animal and the energy it consumes. The research focuses on efficiency. The condor wins. It's the animal that uses the least energy in travelling a mile. The human being was at the bottom of the ranking. But somebody had the idea to redo the experiment with a man on a bicycle. With this tool, man ranked first, far ahead of the condor. Steve Jobs concluded that a computer's purpose was to augment our intellectual abilities, a bit like how a bicycle augments our physical abilities.

This first time, it takes Jobs a good ten minutes to re-count the anecdote. Several years later, invited to shoot a video for the American Library of Congress, Steve Jobs recounts the story once again, but this time in under a minute. He goes right to the point and tells us that, for him, the computer is the most remarkable tool that man has ever created. It's the equivalent of a bicycle for our minds.

79

THE KLONDIKE

I know that the first Apple I is at the Smithsonian museum. To celebrate the production of the millionth Apple II computer, one was made from gold. I don't know if the latter is at Fort Knox.

80

CENTERFOLD

Sometimes you have to accept failure. It happens when you miscalculate. You thought you could get there, but it didn't work out. The difficult thing is figuring out the limit. At which point do you stop yourself? When you've already got the impression of having gone too far, when you already feel tangled up in defeat, how do you find your footing again? The forces of abandon are at work; stay lucid in times of all-out peril.

Only real heroes never give up. That's the part that fascinated Rivages with the story of Steve Jobs. His life is evidence of an iron will, a trajectory never deviated, a set course: create technological products that are easy to use for the most people possible, to make the world a better place. The truth is that he benefits from a story told in hindsight. If he assumes the pose of a hero, it's because Steve Jobs constantly rewrote his own story by taking the best of himself and from others. He used the genius of Steve Wozniak to invent the personal computer. The Apple I is an electronic board conceived to be connected to a keyboard and screen. Two hundred units were produced and sold for $666.66 apiece. Six six six,

the number of the beast who brought success to Iron
Maiden:

Woe to You O Earth and Sea
for the Devil sends the beast with wrath
because he knows the time is short

The Apple I is a success, and the two Steves move
quickly to the conception of their next project. They
must innovate or die. The Apple II comes out in April
1977. It's considered one of the computers that launched
the personal computing market with, among others, the
IBM PC, the TRS-80, and the Commodore PET 2001.

Steve Jobs takes the best elements from others to invent products and write his story. Without Lee Clow
and Steve Hayden, the 1984 ad would have never existed;
without Ridley Scott either. Without Dan Bricklin and
the VisiCalc software, the Apple II would have never sold
more than two million units. VisiCalc is the predecessor
of Microsoft Excel and of all the other software using
spreadsheets. That's what's known as a *killer app*, a software program that becomes a phenomenal success, that
pushes consumers to buy the machine that runs it. VisiCalc
is to Apple II what *Mario Bros.* was for the Nintendo game
console. There's also PostScript, which will launch the
Macintosh into the world of graphic arts. It allows a user
to print onto paper (ideally with an Apple LaserWriter)
exactly what you see onscreen. That's the beginning of
DTP: desktop publishing. PageMaker will also become
an important software program in the history of graphic

design and the Macintosh. We've forgotten it, but at the beginning of the eighties, it's a tour de force, a grand innovation as astounding as the appearance of the mouse to the mainstream public. In the February 1985 issue of *Playboy*, David Sheff, who asks Steve Jobs about the point of a mouse, takes a stab at describing the object to readers: "a little box that is rolled around on your desk and guides a pointer on your computer screen". Jobs responds that, since forever, when we want to show something to someone, we point with our finger. So the mouse is going to take on that function.

Playboy's February 1985 issue contains the most well-known interview with Steve Jobs: "The 29-Year-Old-Zillionaire". But the issue itself is most dedicated to the beautiful ladies of Texas and titled "YAAAA-HOOOOO, It's the Girls of Texas". As such, the blonde with red lips and dazzling teeth on the cover is dressed up as a cowgirl. She wears a handkerchief in America's colors, with white stripes and rabbit logos. White-gloved, she holds a cowboy hat on her head with her left hand. She's standing with her knees slightly crouched, facing the lens at a three-quarter turn. Her leather chaps reveal her bare behind. In the low-cut neckline of her bodice, you admire her left breast. In this issue, Steve Jobs hypothesizes of a near future where a personal computer can connect to a national communication network. He predicts that the PC will dethrone the telephone just as the telephone dethroned the telegraph. The widespread emergence of the web a decade later will substantiate his claims. It reminds us also that the II is a magnificent tool that augments our productivity and creativity. What he doesn't know is that this marvelous communication tool will ultimately eclipse *Playboy* and give birth to the digital sex industry. One quarter of Google searches today are related to porn. Even in the early days of France's Minitel, the adult-chat pink messaging services were the most used feature. In lieu of HD color photos and video streaming, the Minitel drew nude girls with green-cultured zeros and ones on a black screen. When he succeeded at creating the first integrated circuit at Texas Instruments on September 12, 1958, Jack Kilby could have never imagined that his silicon chip would results in the viewing of millions of silicon breasts.

The year of the Jobs interview in *Playboy*, Claude Simon receives the Nobel Prize for literature. Evoking a life filled with experiences, he concludes his acceptance speech with these words: "I have never yet, in seventy-two years, found any sense in all of this, that—as Barthes borrowed from Shakespeare, I believe—'if the world signifies something, it's that it means nothing, except what it is.'"

The cover girl in the cowboy hat with her butt cheeks in the air is named Julie McCullough. The following year, she is Miss February 1986 and fills the center spread. In red boots and a nondescript uniform, she'd finally attained the title of *Playboy Centerfold*.

81

TARZAN "LA BOTTINE" TYLER

Saturday afternoons with my cousin Luc, I often watched wrestling on TV. Our favorite wrestler was, without question, André the Giant. We hated Maurice "Mad Dog" Vachon and we didn't like Tarzan "La Bottine" Tyler much either. We watched the matches on my grandmother's big black-and-white TV set. Before turning it on, we had to let it warm up. We pressed a first button and waited about a minute. Next, we pressed another button, and the image appeared slowly. We could also try to turn it on without letting it warm up, but an adult would yell at us that we'd break the TV and then we wouldn't have it anymore and that would be the end for us....

In those days, in order to function, the tubes of a television set needed to warm up. An electric current made them glow and, once they were hot enough, they could play their role. They were the centerpieces of the circuit. They would soon be replaced by transistors.

Today, TVs no longer warm up, and they are no longer furniture we can decorate with a little lace table skirt, a flower vase, an ashtray, the daily newspaper and the car keys. Today, I no longer watch wrestling and Tarzan "La Bottine" Tyler slowly faded away, like the last television set tubes of our childhood.

82

CONRAD

In the village where my mom and dad were born, everyone had a nickname, and half the nicknames of the villagers there began by Ti, like Ti-Pite, Ti-Jo, Ti-Georges, Ti-Dé, Ti-Frette, Ti-Bod, Ti-Jean, Ti-Gus, Ti-Claude, Ti-Sis, Ti-Mile, Ti-Plam, Ti-Von and quite a few more. My grandfather was Ti-Co.

83

THE BABY BOOK

It's a hardbound album. It looks great. It's something important, the official book of the beginning of your child's life. Here's where you'll keep the traces of all the firsts. Baby is born on… Baby weighs… Baby measures fifty-three centimeters. The names of the baby's parents. Notes: his hair is chestnut brown, his eyes are a very deep blue, for the moment. They're large and very brilliant. His eyebrows are blond, his lashes chestnut brown. The first gifts the baby receives. The baby's photo is on the first page. First trip to a restaurant at thirteen months. He stands up for the first time at eleven months. At a year and a half, he walks very well. He says "papa" on… He says "mama" on… His first tooth appears on Thursday, July 21, the day Armstrong walked on the Moon. "One small step for man, one giant leap for mankind." At sixteen months, he has sixteen teeth, speaks many words, climbs on everything, and doesn't have a very good disposition. He doesn't speak often but understands everything.

Then we leave some blanks. We don't have the time to always keep updating it. We wanted to fill all the pages, but the days all pass very quickly. So we stow away the album somewhere. We place it with the photo albums. We allow the memories to live with other memories. We let time pass until the day we rediscover it. The son opens it up and reads the words written by his mother:

> To my son,
> If you are strong to the point that nothing can trouble your serenity,
> if you instill your friends with confidence in themselves,
> if you forget the mistakes that have passed and look to make a better future,
> if you are too considerate to worry about yourself, too noble to be irritated, too strong to be afraid, and too happy to be troubled, then you'll become a man, my son, and I'll be proud of you.

I believe that's taken from *Meditations* by Marcus Aurelius, who writes in Chapter Sixteen of Book One: "From my adoptive father, I learned kindness; the unshakeable steadfastness in judgments that were once ripe with reflection; the contempt for false honors that seduced his vanity…"

When my son was born, I wrote this: "I am bursting, I hurt all over, but these are the days of my deepest happiness, something so incredible that you can't, even if you wanted to, imprint the current of feeling for this child, from his mother and me a cry of joy from a body, from pores, faced with a nose that quivers, its quick whistle, its hiccups of ecstasy and the ends of language that spread it out. You arrived with the forceps of the moment by following the slope of your parents' endless days."

Fatherhood, at the beginning, is a bit like a drug, rendering you completely delirious.

84

STORYTELLING

At the end of his life, Steve Jobs asks the former director of CNN and *Time* magazine, Walter Isaacson, to write his biography. It's published some time after his death and sells millions of copies. It's a true compendium that borrows from many previously published documents. Since the eighties, Jobs has been the subject of numerous books, as has Apple. If he'd written all the books that speak of him, Jobs would be one of the most prolific authors of the twentieth and twenty-first centuries. Some examples:

- *The Innovation Secrets of Steve Jobs: 7 Principles to Think Differently*
- *The Presentation Secrets of Steve Jobs*
- *The Four Lives of Steve Jobs*
- *The Truth About Steve Jobs*
- *The Life of Steve Jobs: Steve Jobs, the Events of his Life*
- *How Steve Jobs Changed the World*
- *Steve Jobs: The Life of a Genius*
- *Apple Pixar Mania*
- Steve lost his job
- Etc.

From religious wars to great revolutions, from the fall of empires to scientific discoveries, from Buddha to Gandhi, from Santa Claus to Neil Armstrong, from Gutenberg to Einstein, we are always, above all else, a story. Descartes got it wrong. It's not enough to think in order to exist; you have to also say something. That's why he wrote his *Discourse on the Method*. That's why Steve Jobs wanted his biography. I recount, therefore I am.

85

SIGMUND

If Sigmund Freud came back to Earth today, I'd take the plane to Vienna. If Sigmund Freud came back today, I'd search for him until I found him. When Sigmund Freud is finally standing in front of me, I'll punch him in the face. And while he's bent over in two, clutching his bloody nose in his hands, I'll tell him, "Why the hell do we need to know why we act the way we do, if we have no choice in the matter?"

86

IT'S ALL IN THE RHYTHM

I am your father. Ta dah!
Yes, but I, I am the brother of your sister. Tadadah!

87

TRIMETHOXYPHENETHYLAMINE

Twenty years later, I still remember my only trip on mesc like it was yesterday. We'd bought what was available: a small baggy of white powder. There were three of us, and six lines on the table. We rolled a dollar bill and drank beers. When one of us realized that it seemed we were on our way to play hockey in the neighbor's driveway at three in the morning completely naked, we understood that the powder had had an effect.

You find trimethoxyphenethylamine in peyote. Its consumption leads to the distortion of perceptions and judgment.

88

BRIDGE OF SIGHS

Tomorrow, we leave for Venice. We're ready to break. For the past two weeks. Our one-year-old son has been waking up every night, three to four times per night. It's exhausting: to get up, give the bottle to baby, soothe baby, put baby to bed, baby starts crying again, retake baby, re-soothe baby, put baby to bed again, baby cries again, and so on. At one point, I left him to cry for at least fifteen minutes. It was horrible. I managed to calm him down. At around five in the morning, he began to doze off. I wasn't able to fall back asleep.

Yesterday, at some point during the night, as I held my son in my arms and tried to make him sleep, I thought of my ancestors. I got to thinking about those who had come before me and had since disappeared. With my son nestled in my arms in the middle of the night, I understood that it was a tribute to the dead. A revelation. I felt profoundly what we sometimes say: that the dead live among the living. All those extinguished lives; the more I thought about it, the more I remembered them and the more I saw them perpetuated within the life of my son, in his skin of my skin. I realized that, around me, all these people I'd known were always there, next to me, because I'd known them, and they would be carried forward by my son: a continuity of mind and body. It also made me want to read Jung. But tomorrow we leave for Venice and we're going to visit the Bridge of Sighs.

89

GOING TO CALIFORNIA

Estimated arrival time: 12:39. Distance remaining: 2973 km. Rivages will be in Los Angeles in four hours. Ground speed: 859 km/h. Altitude: 11 km. Names appear at random on the Geo Vision map: Baffin Island, Edmonton, Calgary, Regina, Minot, Winnipeg, Fort Berthold Indian Reservation, The Pass, Big Sand Lake, Thompson, Gillam… He reads an article that says that the TV, far from having plunged us into a world of individualism, has instead turned us into a herd. On his iPod, Led Zeppelin sings:

> *Made up my mind to make a new start,*
> *Going to California with an aching in my heart.*
> *Someone told me there's a girl out there*
> *With love in her eyes and flowers in her hair.*
> *Took my chances on a big jet plane,*
> Never let 'em tell you that they're all the same…

At forty years old, he flies over North America. He looks out the plane's window, at the tops of clouds. Led Zep now plays "Moby Dick". It's said that in concert, John Bonham could stretch out the drum solo as long as forty minutes.

Rivages is in Los Angeles for a convention. He finally spots the white letters along the mountain: HOLLYWOOD. Thanks to shock-rocker Alice Cooper, who led a campaign to save the steel letters, the sign is still there. Peg Entwistle killed herself by jumping off the "H" in 1932. Over Venice Beach, Rivages thinks of Jim Morrison. After the convention, he takes a tour of the city in a minibus for tourists: Sunset Boulevard, Rodeo Drive, the Beverly Hills hotel (the one on the cover of *Hotel California* by The Eagles), the home of Marilyn Monroe, that of Tom Cruise and so on. On the Walk of Fame, he walks along all the handprints until he arrives at those of Weissmuller. He's disappointed to not see Cheeta's two paws right next to them. *Cheeta* was named after a cheetah. He's never understood why anyone would give that name to a monkey. He also doesn't know why Apple gave this same name to the first version of its Mac OS X operating system:

Version 10.0: *Cheetah*
Version 10.1: *Puma*
Version 10.2: *Jaguar*
Version 10.3: *Panther*
Version 10.4: Tiger
Version 10.5: *Leopard*
Version 10.6: *Snow Leopard*
Version 10.7: *Lion*
Version 10.8: *Mountain Lion*

Maybe one day they'll get to a version called *White Whale.*

After the tour of the city, he walks back to his hotel. In front of a bar, a young man in a Kings baseball cap asks him if he wants some weed. Why not, how much is it? Upon returning to his room, Number 14, first floor, he rolls a joint. He turns on the TV. He sets up three pillows at the top of the bed to make a spongy recliner. He sits back, legs stretched out. He lights the joint. He surfs, hops, going from one channel to the next: music videos, weather, CNN, black-and-white film, talk show, *Simpsons*, *Seinfeld*. He stops at *Seinfeld*. It reminds him of his year in Toronto. Kramer's entries, those were something, veritable eruptions. Millions tuned in every Thursday for the latest episode. On the desk in his apartment, Jerry had a Macintosh Classic. He never used it, but the Mac was there. Had Apple paid for the product placement?

The weed is good. It quickly goes to his head. He continues with the surfing, the hopping. He's cold. He's thirsty. He returns to the black-and-white film. A man says to a woman, "It's a drop of two hundred feet. He can't do it. He'll kill himself." At that moment, Tarzan dives off the Brooklyn Bridge. Rivages took his time figuring out that it was a Tarzan film because Weissmuller's in clothes, it all takes place in New York, and also because, more and more, he's freezing. He goes to get a beer from the minibar and a packet of peanuts. He shouldn't have gotten up so quickly. His head is spinning. The buzz is at its peak. He downs the beer. On the screen, a host says something about an ad. He's talking about computers. He's going to show us Captain Kirk introducing the Commodore Vic-20. Next, we see the first portable computer from Big Blue in 1977, the IBM 5100. There's also Bill Cosby for Texas Instruments, Alan Alda on behalf of Atari, and Dick Cavett for Apple. Rivages goes to get another beer, rolls a cigarette. The host of the show who's stringing together the timeline of TV ads for computers now interviews Steve Hayden, one of the creators of the 1984 ad. Hayden explains that people believed Big Brother represented IBM, but that wasn't the goal of the message. The ad wanted to break the myth of technology as invasive and oppressive. What they wanted to show was that the personal computer was an emancipatory force that led to more freedom. Rivages is about to flip the channel again but he stops. The review of IBM's ads puts Chaplin's The Tramp up on the screen. He's forgotten this moment. Several memories floated back. IBM is The Tramp, Big Blue is the vagrant, it's like watching flashbacks of people in their youth. He must've been ten years old then. It's far away, all this. What's left of it? His heart hurts. He shouldn't have smoked whatever he'd bought in the street from some stranger a thousand miles from home. The Tramp is happy to have a personal computer. His life is pretty magnificent, worry-free, all goes well, he's saved by the machine. And Rivages can no longer look at the screen, it hurts his eyes. He feels asphyxiated. He tells himself that it's been forty years that he's been in front of a screen, that of the TV, that of the movies, that of a computer, and now that of his phone. His head spins faster and faster. Something inside him comes undone, his anguish rising, pressing down on the pit of his plexus. He turns toward the nightstand. He takes the bottle. He drinks the last sip of beer. What's he doing in this room? What's he doing in the city of angels? He studies the bottle in his hand, he looks at the TV screen. A blonde woman in red shorts and a white T-shirt runs. She's pursued by an anti-riot squad. Big Brother speaks on a large screen. She spins her body and throws a sledgehammer at the screen. With the same motion, Rivages launches his beer bottle with all his might into the television. The cathode tube explodes with a deafening bang. There's a knock at the door. Someone's trying to open it. It's the hotel's concierge. He opens up and finds Rivages vomiting all over the carpet at the side of the bed. The screen is in shards, the room stinks of marijuana and fried circuitry. Between two heaves, Rivages manages to say, "Fuck Steve Jobs!"

90

FLUTTERS

I love my son so much that when I think of him I get butterflies in my stomach. It's like when I was little and I was in the car on Sundays, and we went to eat at my grandparents, I would ask my dad, at the point where the road buckles into a bump, to accelerate so I could get the flutters in my stomach. Often, to please me, my father made a U-turn so we could go over the bump again at full speed. My son, sometimes, gives me the same sensation.

91

MAC OR PC

Are you Mac or PC? Those who haven't participated in this type of conversation at least once in their lives weren't thirty years old in the year 2000. I'm not really exaggerating. It was always a major topic of discussion. You chose your camp and you had to be ready to defend it, whether you were up to it or not. The Mac was criticized for its price. But it was beautiful. The Mac was criticized for its closed system, but when you connected something to it, it worked the very first time. That wasn't the case for PCs where the smallest material addition was complicated. The interface was equally less meticulous. Windows was nothing but a pale facsimile of what Apple had been proposing for years. It was often at this point that the knockout argument landed: yeah, but on a Macintosh, there were no games. Once an adversary had said that, for him, the case was won. You could always try to tell him that games on computers didn't interest you, which for him was only a declaration of bad faith.

92

POWERPOINT

PowerPoint is one of the best-known software programs from the Microsoft Office suite, alongside Word and Excel. It allows a user to assemble together on a computer different texts, images, and graphics, as well as sound and video. PowerPoint pages are also called diapositives. The reference is to an old analog system composed of a projector that had a carousel made of black plastic, in which one never knew which way to place the diapositives, and a rotating screen that went Zviiiiiiittttt clack! when you switched the image from one to the next.

PowerPoint is a layout-design program developed for presentations on computer screens or office video projectors or at convention centers. You can also print out a PowerPoint presentation, though it is strongly advised against distributing it to audiences before the presentation. They will have a tendency to read rather than listen to you.

Over time, PowerPoint has become a powerful tool. Those who perfectly master PowerPoint can convince others of practically anything. Legend has it that Steve Jobs was the most masterful user of PowerPoint ever. From 2003, he insisted that Apple develop its own presentation software, first for his personal use and then for commercialization under the name Keynote. The secret to a successful presentation is the following:

Use nine diapositives.
Separate the presentation into three parts of three
    pages each.
Separate the three parts into three sub-parts. ·
Use only one single image per diapositive.
The length of the presentation should not exceed
    twenty minutes.
One should inform, educate, and entertain.
One should tell a story.

93

TOOTHBRUSH

At bedtime, I'm in the habit of telling my son: pipi, teeth,
dodo. Sometimes, so he doesn't forget his Québécois
roots, I tell him: pisse pis couche (pee then sleep). But he
still has to go brush his teeth.

94

SEVENTY-FOUR DAYS

It's an enormous sequoia. The first time they passed by there, the Spanish thought "tree" and "large", palo and alto. Today it's the name of a city. Bill and Dave founded Hewlett-Packard and launched what would become Silicon Valley. It was also in this neck of California that the Stanfords decided to build a university after the death of their son. Leland Stanford Junior is fifteen years old when he succumbs to typhoid fever in 1884 during a trip to Italy. His father, one of the richest men in the United States, once governor of California, director of Wells Fargo, founder of the Central Pacific Railroad, reportedly stated, "We've lost our son, henceforth all the children of California shall be our children." He invests part of his fortune into the service of education and teaching. Today, Stanford is considered one of the best universities in the world.

On June 12, 2005, thousands of students gathered with their parents and friends in the university's stadium. More than twenty thousand people attended the institution's one hundred and fourteenth graduation convocation. The ceremony began with a presentation by the guest of honor. That guest is Steve Jobs. The lecture he gives that day, which would become the most infamous of all his presentations, is now known as "The Stanford Lecture".

Jobs begins by saying that he's there simply to recount three stories from his life. He'll speak of destinies, life, love and death.

In the first story, he relates episodes from his life and asks how he can make sense of them. He speaks of an adopted child, the invention of character fonts on the Macintosh, and the need to write his own story. He says that he must believe in something. It's important to persuade yourself that the events of our lives will one day form a coherent ensemble. It's like those drawings where you must connect the dots by following the numbers. At the beginning, we can't see where we're going, but closer to the end a meaning emerges. When he was small, Rivages's son loved connecting the dots. Jobs insists: you must believe in something.

The second story is about his dismissal from Apple. It was a bitter failure for him. But he didn't lose faith. Like Christ in the desert, he remained steadfast to his purpose. You have to hang on to your passion. To do so, you have to be passionate about what you do. Any if you haven't yet found it, don't stop looking, continue. Finally, he concludes with the story of his illness. He brings up a catchphrase that draws laughter from the crowd: "If you live each day as if it's your last, one day you'll have a reason." Then, as he knows what he's doing, he starts talking about death and increases the tension. He grabs the attention and emotion of the audience. It's no longer

Steve Jobs on the stage, but a priest at a pulpit, a preacher atop a mountain who says, "Remember that one day you're going to die. You've got nothing to lose. Live your life. Be free. Follow your heart and your intuition, as they already know who you really want to be."

The grand priest descends back down to earth. In his black robe, Jobs talks about the Whole Earth Catalog, the bible for hippies, which was a kind of paper-version Google published by fanatics advocating the barter system across America. The final volume of the catalogue ends on these words: "Stay hungry, stay foolish." This is what Jobs advises all the Stanford graduates in the guise of a conclusion.

Steve Jobs is a motivator, a guru, a preacher without dogma: each individual is responsible for his own happiness, it's all but a question of will. It's as beautiful, as grand, as formidable, and probably as true as the creation of the world in seven days. But it works. Steve promises us happiness that doesn't call for anything other than ourselves. He liberates us from society. The computer is the perfect tool for this emancipation. He gives us the possibility to be who we want to be. When she throws her sledgehammer into the screen and blows up Big Brother, Anya Mayor liberates us all. In 1984, Apple had projected to sell 50,0000 Macintosh computers in the span of one year. They ended up selling 50,000 in seventy-four days.

95

UNDERSTAND

- ◆ "Why do you write?
- ◆ To understand.
- ◆ So?
- ◆ I don't understand.
- ◆ Write harder!"

96

ELECTRIC BATTERY

Laboulaye imagined it. Bartholdi drew it. Viollet-le-Duc and Eiffel built it. Work began in Paris in 1875 in the Monduit, Gaget & Gauthier workshop. During nine years they cut, drill, screw, hammer, pull, coil, assemble. The statue slowly emerges from the ground. It dominates over the rooftops of Paris. Next it crosses the Atlantic Ocean in pieces and is raised facing New York in 1886.

If you dunk copper and iron in saltwater, it creates a chemical reaction, like in an electric battery. The Statue of Liberty, made of iron and copper, once erected amidst the saltwater of the Atlantic, reacts chemically like an electric battery. The symbol of America is electric. From Edison to Jobs, the electron has given birth to an empire.

I have a friend who doesn't like the United States. For him, the Statue of Liberty is a tombstone that reads: here lies liberty! I enjoy his company because he always takes extreme positions.

97

NATURE ISN'T PERFECT

Yesterday evening, my son went to bed saying he wasn't tired. He said he didn't feel like sleeping. This morning, my son had a hard time getting out of bed. He wanted to keep sleeping. Drinking his hot cocoa, he told me again that he'd rather keep sleeping. I told him it was often a problem: in the evening, we don't want to sleep, then come morning we don't want to get up. I told him it would all be much simpler if in the evening we wanted to sleep and in the morning we wanted to get up. My son of ten years looked up from his hot cocoa. He looked at me as if I was naïve and said, "Nature isn't perfect."

98

ROCK 'N' ROLL

Emil Nobel dies on September 3, 1864, while handling liquid nitroglycerine. His brother Alfred decides to find a solution for the dangers inherent with this unstable substance. Dynamite is patented in 1867. Thanks to this new explosive, goldmines in California can be dug up that much faster. Beneath the mountains, tunnels advance at top speeds. In war, a single stick of dynamite does the work of many soldiers. Alfred Nobel becomes rich, very rich. But the death of his brother and that of millions of innocent people ends up weighing on his conscience. That's why he decides to bequeath his fortune to the creation of a foundation. Each year, this organization rewards the work of the men and women who've contributed, in an exemplary manner, to the evolution of humanity.

For their research on semi-conductors and their discovery of the transistor effect, William Bradford Shockley, John Bardeen and Walter Houser Brattain receive the Nobel Prize in Physics in 1956. The first product developed from the transistor is the Regency pocket radio. It isn't immediately clear how this would contribute to the evolution of humanity. However, once you know that the transistor gives birth to electronic chips and that it's the seed of modern computing, you understand it a little better.

Walter Brattain once said that his only regret regarding the transistor, was that he'd aided in the spread and popularity of rock & roll.

99

SOCRATES 2.0

Socrates never wrote a single word. It was Plato who wrote down what Socrates said. In Phaedrus, Plato recounts an encounter between Socrates and Phaedrus. They converse along the bank of a river. Socrates shares with Phaedrus the legend of Toth, an Egyptian god. He's given the traits of an ibis or a baboon. He invents numbers, geometry, astronomy, games of chance, and language. It's said that one day Toth paid a visit to King Thamos to tell him that writing was a very useful invention, to which the king replied, "It can only produce, in souls, the oblivion of what they know by making them forget. Because if they will have faith in writing, it is by what's outside, by foreign impressions, and not from within and from their own depths, that men will seek to remember. You have found the cure (pharmakon), not to enrich the memory, but to preserve the memories it has. You give your disciples the presumption that they control science, not that science controls itself. When, indeed, they have learned much without a master, they will imagine themselves as very learned, and they will for the most part be the ignorants of inconvenient commerce, imaginary scholars (*doxosophoi*) instead of true scholars."

It's like being on a TV show where one of the guests, an *expert philosopher*, explains why the web is leading humanity to ruin. At one time, it was called the information highway.

100

DEEP BLUE

Around 1950, the world's most renowned scientists were still speculating over the probability that, one day maybe, we'd be capable of building a computer capable of playing a few turns in a chess match against a human being. In 1997, IBM's Deep Blue beat Garry Kasparov, the world champion of chess, in their second series of six-game matches.

When a man can no longer tell the difference between a machine and a man, it's not the man who becomes the machine, but the machine that becomes the man. According to Turing, we are perhaps only the result of a complex algorithm.

FIRST BE BEST, THEN BE FIRST

Apple is:
    the first personal computer,
    the first graphic interface,
    the first commercial mouse,
    the first color screen,
universal copy/paste between applications,
    the first computer with an icon that smiles at you while loading
    the first rolling menu,
    the first all-in-one computer with integrated screen and central processing unit,
    and the first CEO who becomes a superstar and who ascends to an iconic status in the popular culture equivalent to that of a Hollywood celebrity or rock star.

AMNESIA

In 1966, France launches Plan Calcul. It's a national re-search and computing program. General de Gaulle under-stood the importance of the computer. Having an atom bomb wasn't enough. The power of a country resides also in its capacity to master super-calculators. The creation of the National Institute of Research in Information and Automation (INRIA) is part of Plan Calcul. Today, thirty-four hundred researchers work there to "invent tomorrow's digital technologies that interface with the informational sciences and mathematics".

For the fortieth anniversary of the Institute, Michel Serres hosts a conference. Like Norbert Wiener before him with cybernetics, he considers the world through the rubric of communication. He says that all organisms, all objects, store, treat, and exchange information. He says that before the invention of writing, information passed through the bodies of human beings: gestures, speech, mind, exchange. With the advent of writing, information separated from the body. Man could store outside himself. Writing replaces the memory. Writing exchanges with other writing. The first cities are born. Geometry is invented. Monotheisms, known as the religions of the Book, rise and take their place in the social conscience.

The philosopher says that writing is a modification of the connection between a message and its medium. He says that with writing, the medium of the message is the slab of wood, the wax plate, papyrus, paper. He says that the invention of the printing press by Gutenberg is another modification in the relationship between medium and message. He says that, today, the human memory is outside of people. He says that the new technologies of information liberate the human being. He says that, liberated from his memory, man will make better use of his imagination.

103

WYSIWYG

In his speech at the Nobel Prize ceremony, Walter Houser Brattain touches upon the importance of surfaces. It's true that we don't think often enough about surfaces. Yet, that's where we live, on the surface of Earth. Most chemical reactions are produced on the surface of the body. It's essentially on the surface of a plant that light transforms into energy. In electronics, most if not all the active elements of a circuit depend on the phenomenon of disequilibrium on the surface of matter. It's not me who says this, it's Brattain. He adds that biology is equally a history of surface interactions. Sight, our most important sense, allows us to perceive surfaces. When we touch someone, it's also surface contact.

I believe that the story of Steve Jobs can also be found on the surface. His biggest credo was: the interior is as important as the exterior. He constructed his life on this idea. That said, I think that even if he was always a prick in his relations with people, it's because he'd decided to put no boundary between what he thought and what he said. For Jobs, the interface, which we can also call the intersurface, must be transparent. That's where his taste for all that's encased in glass comes from, which he illustrates in the design of Apple Stores, done completely in glass.

WYSIWYG is the acronym for the slogan, "What you see is what you get". It's thanks to WYSIWYG that computers were made available to the public at large. Among other reasons, it's thanks to its graphic interface that the Macintosh became a mythic machine.

104

PAPER MATE FLAIR

One day, they replaced my Paper Mate 0.5 pen with a
Paper Mate Flair M New Design, writing that's clear and
bright, a soft felt tip, comes in sizes fine (F), medium
(M), and bold (B). Reference EU FLR RFRSHFTP M.BLK,
barcode 008285095126. MADE IN MEXICO.

- Ideal for day-to-day writing and drawing.
- Continuous, unbroken line.
- Water-based ink that doesn't bleed on the paper.
Newell Rubbermaid™—Brands That Matter.

"Clear and bright writing": I told myself I've got nothing to lose.

105

WHAT'S THE CONNECTION?

What's the connection between Steve Jobs and Alan Turing? What's the connection between Steve Jobs and I Ching? What's the connection between Steve Jobs and Mark I? What's the connection between Steve Jobs and Ross Perot? What's the connection between Steve Jobs, Einstein, and Thomas Edison? What's the connection between Steve Jobs and a Nobel Prize in Physics? What's the connection between Steve Jobs and the Statue of Liberty? What's the connection between Jobs and Orwell? What's the connection between Ridley Scott and Snow White? What's the connection between Woody Allen and Maurice Richard? What's the connection between a Selectronic writing machine and Steve Jobs? What's the connection between Tarzan, Brautigan, and Jobs? What's the connection between the mouse and Frankenstein? What's the connection between Bob Dylan and Claviceps purpurea? What's the connection between Hiroshima and the transistor? The connection is that all of these objects and all of the people are part of the same story.

106

MERCEDES BENZ

A teenager lost in the middle of Texas, Janis Joplin finds a job to make some pocket money. With the help of a hole punch, she makes holes in cards. For several months, she makes perforated cards for computers. She transcribes computer programs, as well as duplicates them. In the sixties, before magnetic tape, diskettes, USB keys and external hard-drives, that's how it was done. Computers were piloted by perforated cards. Janis is a modern version of the old ticket puncher in Serge Gainsbourg's song, "Le poinçonneur des Lilas". But the rebellious young girl quits the assembly-line job for music, and Texas for California. She won't be an IBM slave and the name of her first band has nothing to do with the Apple ad: Big Brother and the Holding Company!

Janis Joplin said somewhere that being an intellectual creates a lot of questions, but not many answers. You can have a headful of theory and still go home to sleep alone. The only thing you have that really counts is your feelings. That's the whole essence of music:

> *Oh Lord, won't you buy me a Mercedes Benz?*
> *My friends all drive Porsches, I must make amends.*

Worked hard all my lifetime, no help from my friends,
So Lord, won't you buy me a Mercedes Benz?

107

THE NEXT BIG REVOLUTION

In the years when LSD is still freely sold, in that time when the hippies revel in the Summer of Love, engineers work in their laboratories near San Francisco. They'd completed their studies in mathematics, in physics, in electronic engineering. As part of projects financed by NASA and the US Army, they conduct experiments. They use the latest technological discoveries and tinker with robots, machines to calculate, to communicate. Their research center is called the Stanford Research Institute. Inside this institute, there's a team known as SAIL, the Stanford Artificial Intelligence Laboratory. The men and women who work there in complete freedom firmly believe that computing can augment the intellectual capacity of humans. Their leader is Doug Engelbart. They can take credit for the invention of the mouse, among other things. They can also take credit for the development of the ARPANET network, which will become the Internet. Many of the Institute's researchers would later work at Xerox PARC.

All this happens near San Francisco in the sixties, between Palo Alto, Mountain View, Redwood, Sunnyvale,

196

Cupertino, and Menlo Park. Not the town of Menlo Park in New Jersey, which became Edison Township, but the city of Menlo Park in California. They both nevertheless take their name from an old Irish sixteenth-century castle built on the banks of the Corrib river. Today, Menlough Castle is an ivy-covered ruin.

This corner of California is reaching its boiling point. While teams at the Institute spend their nights glued to their screens, youth from across the country are showing up in Frisco for a taste of free love and to reach nirvana through utter stonedom, easily and inexpensively. They march against segregation and for equality, for a new life and against the war. The ball gets rolling at the University of California. A certain Fred Moore decides to occupy a corner of the campus, to give speeches and to distribute leaflets against the American activities in Cambodia. For John Markoff, Moore's sit-in is the founding act in the revolt of the sixties. Markoff is the author of *What the Dormouse Said: How the Sixties Counterculture Shaped the Personal Computer Industry,* Penguin Books, 2005, 310 pages. After the Cuban missile crisis, Fred Moore takes part in the March for Peace in Quebec, Washington, and Cuba. The march leaves from Quebec City on May 26, 1963, and lasts more than one year. All along its course, numerous incidents are protested. When the demonstrations are about to cross from Florida to Castro's island, they're stopped by the police. That's the end of the *Quebec-Washington-Gauntánamo Walk for Peace.*

After having demonstrated against the American presence in Cambodia and Vietnam, against Nixon and his vice-president Spiro Agnew, Fred Moore the pacifist turns to computing. It will be his new warhorse: computers for all! Ordinary folks should seize upon this science in the process of being born. It's in this spirit that he founds, with Gordon French, the Homebrew Computer Club. Electronics and computer hobbyists from the area show up and discuss, sharing their latest experiments. That's where Steve Jobs and Steve Wozniak make their debut. While on the East coast the Massachusetts Institute for Technology and Bell laboratories and IBM continue to develop gigantic computers for the needs of the military and large enterprise, visionaries from the West coast try to create machines at the human level capable of being used by anyone. Jim Warren, Larry Tesler, John McCarthy, and Alan Kay are among those taking part. Kay's most famous saying is, "The best way to predict the future is to invent it."

Dreamers, hippies, and scientists mix with each other on the peninsula of San Francisco. In 1961, the International Foundation for Advanced Study opens its doors just a few steps from the Stanford Research Institute at Menlo Park. Myron Stolaroff manages to secure several grants to conduct experiments with LSD and mescaline. Nearly 350 people show up for a trip under the surveillance of researchers who observe, question, and study. For them, LSD, acid, and mescaline appear to have the power to carry the spirit toward new horizons. Ever since the experiment described by Aldous Huxley in *The Doors of Perception*, America wants its dose. It's as a tribute to this philosophical essay that Morrison, Manzarek, Krieger, and Densmore decide to call themselves The Doors.

It's said that a number of the Institute's scientists, including its director Doug Engelbart, participate in Stolaroff's experiments. In effect, the two organizations have the same goal, the augmentation of a human's intellectual capacities. The engineers look to arrive there by computer, the psychologists by psychotropics. At the time, the American military is also conducting its own clinical studies on LSD. It tests combat brigades under the effect of the drug in the hope of better controlling their minds. The results are lamentable. Hundreds of soldiers in the exercise fall apart, overtaken with crazed laughter or muscle spasms. The CIA even goes so far as to test the product on a large scale on the population of a village in the south of France in 1951. Code name: MKUltra. The French press report the event as follows, "The hallucinators in Pont-Saint-Esprit seem to be suffering from Ergotism. Thirty of the sick, from the one-hundred-and-fifty intoxicated by the bad bread of Pont-Saint-Esprit, become crazed and need to be interned."

During an LSD experiment organized by Stolaroff, the Institute's engineers are asked to invent something. Of the ten completely stoned scientists, only one is capable of performing the exercise. As colors spiraled, walls swayed, and episodes of vomiting overwhelmed them, one scientist imagines a miniature hydraulic mill that could be installed within the depths of a toilet. When a man is pissing, he must aim at the blades of the mill so they turn. The inventor explains that this device will allow training individuals of the masculine sex to not pee on the toilet seat. The evaluators conclude that

LSD is not a very conducive substance when it comes to technological innovation.

In another study, Stolaroff focuses on perception. Guinea pigs filled out a questionnaire, the study sought statistics. The results show that a large number of respondents feel more receptive to their environment, more open and advantaged by a communion with others also under the effect of LSD. Steve Jobs never took this test, but his story carries within it this influence of California's counter-culture of the sixties and seventies. If he's able to adopt the pose of a locust, a Macintosh computer balanced on his legs, it's because Steve Jobs is a son of the Aquarian Age. There's no cheating in life. He manages to convince himself, and convince a good part of the planet, that what he conceived is a benefit for humanity. By dint of succeeding and rebounding, despite being unlikeable, he becomes popular. He's cited as an exemplar. Too bad if he's also a bastard who for years refuses to recognize his own paternity. Too bad if he's a millionaire prick who refuses to help the mother of his child. Too bad if he gives a machine the name of his daughter, Lisa, instead of taking an interest in her. Too bad if the Apple boss is a little crazy and decides to call his youngest daughter Eve. He went to Reed College in Oregon, and his son gets Reed as a name. He always claimed to be Zen and owned a private jet. Anyway, computing won and psychedelic drugs lost. All we have left are graphic animations in iTunes to try to imagine an evening on acid in Golden Gate Park in 1967 with the Grateful Dead, Janis Joplin, and Richard Brautigan.

It's said that, as a teenager, Jobs read *Moby Dick*, listened to Bob Dylan and recited Dylan Thomas. For a guy his age in 1973, it wasn't very original. However, later on, he has a relationship with Joan Baez, which is a little more unique.

For some, the first micro-computer was invented in France by Francois Gernelle in 1972. This would be the Micral. There was also Osborne I, the Dynabook, the Xerox Alto, the Altair 8800, etc. So many machines that have advanced computer technology, so many machines that imposed upon us their descendants. It appears that, in 1969, David Evans and Steward Brand hosted Ken Kesey at Stanford's Artificial Intelligence Laboratory. When they showed him what they could do with a computer, the leader of the Merry Pranksters, the father of acid tests, the future author of *One Flew Over the Cuckoo's Nest*, exclaimed, "This is the next big revolution after acid!"

108

SNAPSHOT OF THE TIMES

Here's what the Internet looked like in its beginnings in 1982, more precisely on January 26 at 1:50:13 pm:

NEWSGROUP	Description
net.auto owners.	General Information for automobile
net.aviation	General information about aviation.
net.chess	General information about computer chess.
net.columbia	General information on space shuttle and space programs.
net.cycle	General information about motorcycles.
net.games	Information and discussion on computer games.
net.ham-radio operators.	Topics of interest to amateur radio
net.jokes	The latest "good" joke you've heard?
net.lan	Local area network interest group.
net.lsi	Large Scale Integrated Circuit discussions.
net.movies	Movie reviews by members of USENET.
net.music	Computer generated music.
net.news.newsite	To announce a new site.

net.rec	General info on recreational (participation) sports.
net.rec.bridge	Subgroup of net.rec – contract bridge.
net.rec.scuba	Subgroup of net.rec – scuba diving.
net.rec.ski	Subgroup of net.rec – skiing.
net.records	Info and opinions about records (and tapes?).
net.rumor	For posting of rumors.
net.sport	General info about spectator sports.
net.sport.baseball	Subgroup of net.sport – for baseball.
net.sport.football	Subgroup of net.sport – for football.
net.sport.hockey	Subgroup of net.sport – for hockey.
net.taxes	Tax advice and queries.
net.travel	Requests, suggestions, and opinions about traveling.
net.ucds	Circuit drawing system.
Etc.	

It's worth noting that this snapshot has been slightly reframed. It was taken by a certain Curt on January 26, 1982.

109

YOUR TURN

Ever since my son was very little, I accompanied him in the morning. Every day of the week, for three years, I dropped him off at his daycare lady, his nana, around 9 am. At first, I carried him in his car seat to her door. Later, he was able to walk. He'd climb out of the car by giving me his hand. Each morning I kissed him before continuing on my way to work , I held him in my arms, wished him a good day.

The first day of school arrived quickly. We prepared a bag with pens, colored pencils, and notebooks, and we set out proper clothes, new shoes. He was still very little. I had to leave him with the teacher. All day long in the middle of the pack, he was going to have to find his place. It was the beginning of a big stage in his socialization. He was going to have to learn how to make himself known in a group, in relation to other voices, other universes.

I no longer know if he cried that first day. I believe he didn't. For me, just thinking about it, receding from the door of the school as it closes, makes my eyes sting. But we did it. We must always go through with it. We must advance, continue. My son was growing older, my son went to school.

Now that the school is a few steps from our home, I no longer drop him off by car. So, every morning, in good weather and in bad, we walk together on the sidewalk for a few minutes. We've been walking side-by-side, father and son, since the beginning of school, since the beginning of his life. But this morning, we were hardly on our way, he was turning ten in one month, he stopped. He turned toward me.

"Actually, Papa, if I want, I can go to school all by myself now?"

"Of course, my big guy."

"So, can I go all alone this morning?"

"If that's what you want, buddy. I'll watch you cross the street. Be careful. Have a good day."

I gave him a kiss on the cheek while pressing him against me a little harder than usual, pretending I was fine with it. He crossed the street and walked toward the school, all alone. I stood planted there, watching him get farther off, like the big boy he was. I thought of the Little Tramp at the end of the movie, when he walks off into the horizon. I thought of the life that awaited him, the one that he'd have to face himself, a little more alone. I thought of those ten years of watching him grow up, of preparing his baby bottle, of changing his diaper, of telling him stories, of playing with balls, of Lego, of tennis, of baseball, of skiing, of telling jokes, of making forts out of sofa cushions in the living room, of biking, of having fun. I thought of the night rocking him so he'd fall back asleep. I thought of his first nightmares, his first Christmas, his first steps, his first word, "Papa", the first trout he ever fished one Sunday afternoon in June. I saw him again, at a year old, feet in the waves, while we were on vacation. I saw his mouth covered in chocolate ice cream. I saw him laughing loudly in the pool. I saw him on the knees of his grandparents, in the arms of friends. I saw him continue biting into life. I remembered that word he repeated all the time when he was happy: Again! Again! Again!

This morning, when he decided to go to school all by himself, it was this word that kept popping in my head: Again! Again! My eyes got misty. My nose sniffled. I watched him get farther away, unable to move. My son, too big so fast. My, son who'll fall in love and will be hurt. My son, who'll maybe go around the world and never come back. My son in his own life. My son, who'll listen to me politely when I tell him that I'll always be there, that every day of his life, I'll continue to walk on the sidewalk with him, that he can always turn to talk to me, ask for advice or hug me. And when I'm gone, I'll still be there. I am there forever, I am the paternal symbol.

My son is going to be ten years old in a month. This morning, he decided to go to school all by himself. I watched him leave. I hope he will achieve what he defines as desirable. I hope he'll tell a good story. I wish you a son as magnificent as you've been, as the one you are. Now it's your turn to play.

110

GARAGE BAND

America loves success stories that begin in a garage. From rock bands to multinationals, it gives strength to the story. It's the modern version of "Once upon a time a young boy who was very poor…" I would venture to add that the myth of the garage is to the American dream what the myth of the cave is to Western philosophy. Anyway, Apple's beginnings in a garage belonging to the parents of Steve Jobs are not just a good story. It's downright brilliant, almost mythological.

111

JOB OFFER

Description for the position of Specialist:

As a specialist, you embody the essence of the client experience at the Apple Store. You know how to be passionate and inexhaustible about the coolest products in the world. You gain the trust of your interlocutors by recommending solutions that not only meet their immediate needs, but inspire them with new dreams and hopes. And you satisfy your customers by constantly finding new ways to make their purchase even more rewarding.

112

CALIFORNIA DREAMING

A Chinese proverb says, "The journey is the reward."
Steve Jobs really appreciated that. Jeffrey Young made
it the title of the biography he published in 1987: *Steve
Job: The Journey is the Reward*. Walter Isaacson, the
official biographer of the father of the iPhone, used it
as well. The title of his Chapter 13 is "Building the Mac:
The Journey is the Reward". Steve would have used this
maxim to motivate his troops at the beginning of the
Macintosh project in 1981. It's a way of saying that you
have to enjoy life, that the destination is less important
than the path leading to it.

Rivages went in search of Weissmuller, Brautigan
and Jobs, just as thousands of men and women em-
barked on the Oregon Trail, towards California, in the
nineteenth century. They crossed over to a New World
in search of paradise lost. They walked towards their
happiness with carriages containing their lives under
a crushing sun, in barely survivable conditions. They
endured it all even though they had one thousand
reasons to give up, from one moment to the next. Let it
all fall, sit in place, stop moving, simply wait for death in

the heat of the day and the cold of the night, in between cacti, as the wind rises and blends in with the howls of wolves and as the rattlesnakes slide softly across sand that's still hot.

These thousands of men and women continued because they were not alone, because they believed in it, because they wanted to achieve the goal they had set for themselves. Rivages also followed his Oregon trail. It led him to Tarzan, to the last of the beatniks and to the book of Jobs in this California that flooded with gold diggers in the peak seasons of 1849. He followed the trail like the others, eyes riveted on images of a happy life, between laughing children and old men with smiles across their faces. California, the land of plenty where the ocean feeds rivers that feed orchards. Orange groves grow beautiful fruit in this valley where, for centuries, thousands of Native Americans lived. Pioneers massacred them. They took their place. The worm was in the apple. The dream became less pure.

Rivages dreams that he reaches the West Coast. Rivages dreams that he is on the beach. The Pacific laps at the sand before him. In his dream, the sun sets. In his dream, it's the end of the day. In his dream, he finally achieved his goal. In his dream, he's realized all his desires. In his dream, he walks slowly towards the water. In the air, the smells of salt and seaweed surround him. He walks and his feet touch the water. He walks straight ahead. The sun on the horizon pulls him closer. Water laps up to his knees, water to his thighs, water to his genitals, water to his navel, water to his stomach, water to his chest, both arms in the water, his neck then his chin made wet by the waves. His mouth, nose and ears fill with water. Eyes closed, water washes over him. Rivages continues to walk.

Under the influence of LSD, his eyes open, Rivages sees dream sequences projected above him. On the walls of a room divided into cubicles, neon-shaped slogans flash in red, yellow and green: WHAT DOESN'T KILL US MAKES US STRONGER. Or also: FIRST BE BEST, THEN BE FIRST. A letter wheel from a Selectronic writing machine hurtles down the middle of a corridor, leaving behind it a trail of words: THINK DIFFERENT. Then a text begins to unfurl, the one from the Apple TV ad with Gandhi, Einstein, Lennon, and also Seinfeld in his series finale, broadcast in Gothic letters amidst the smoke of the Twin Towers:

> Here's to the crazy ones. The misfits. The rebels. The troublemakers. The round pegs in the square holes. The ones who see things differently. They're not fond of rules. And they have no respect for the status quo. You can quote them, disagree with them, glorify or vilify them. About the only thing you can't do is ignore them. Because they change things. They push the human race forward. While some may see them as the crazy ones, we see genius. Because the people who are crazy enough to think they can change the world, are the ones who do.

It's a bit like the opening text of Michael Radford's *1984*, which hit the silver screen in 1984 to pay homage to

211

Orwell's book and that starred John Hurt and Richard Burton. The latter dies in 1984. Design is not the shape, but the function. The first computer fair on the West coast took place in April 1977. This event marked the birth of the computer industry. Suzanne Kare is the graphic designer who made the Mac smile. She drew all the icons for the operating system, from computer to hard-drive.

In Rivages's delirium, the Statue of Liberty has traded in her torch for a pirates' flag. We work twenty hours a day and we like it. Gabriel sees Moses on the mountain with his Ten Commandments. The ten commandments have been replaced by this text:

> The Front de liberation du Québec is not the Messiah nor a Robin Hood for modern times. It's a gathering of Québécois workers who have decided to put everything on the line so that the people of Quebec can definitively take their own destiny in hand. [R.I.P., October 7, 1970.]

Rivages sees himself take photos with an old Polaroid. He presses the button. Mozart's *Requiem* resounds and a square card falls into his hand. He blows on it for the image to be revealed, and the face of Lisa, the daughter of Jobs, appears. She's thirty years old and she's beautiful. Her father initially rejected her. She is now the heiress of a billionaire.

A closed computing system limits the possibilities of the user, but it is more stable and more predictable. An open system is a lot more fragile and less reliable, that's the price of liberty. To the question Why write?, Beckett replies Because it's as good as anything else, and Sartre says What else can I do? In his hallucination, Rivages sees a gigantic face appear over a mountain. It's not Big Brother. He had large black spectacles, a broad, bare forehead, and a tie. His silhouette bathes the surrounding light. The mountain transforms, mingling with the face in the chaos of colors. It's Benoit Mandelbrot (1924 – 2010), the father of fractals, images of chaos created by computers. The economist-mathematician, a bottle brush in his hand, baptizes the geometric figures of his own invention: the island of von Koch, the snowflake, Cantor dust, Besicovitch's diabolic stairs… In a spasm of LSD colors, he disappears by saying, "I want to find the rules that shape the world, since the ultimate goal of science is to concur with the Great Lord." His face seemingly melts away.

All at once, Rivages cries, "I am the time that, in progressing, destroys the world." The growth of the population implies a decline in the value of human life. Novus Ordo Seclorum. He sees Jarlie Japlin and Chanis Choplin crossing a river on the back of a crocodile whose reins are held by Tarzan. Cheetah and Noam Chomsky throw Frisbees in the shape of zeroes. The linguist says to the monkey, "How can I speak with a machine? The word algorithm comes from the name al-Khwarizmi, a man born in Persia in 783, propagator of the zero and inventor of algebra." Cheetah answers that the secret of happiness is to be resolute, patient, responsible, happy, humble, generous, curious, responsive and original!

Today, Big Brother is the name of a reality TV show. The modern state exists upon a monopoly of the exercise of legitimate violence within its borders and on the actions of a national army outside them. To celebrate the twentieth anniversary of the Macintosh, the 1984 ad was computer-edited, image by image, and an iPod was embedded on the neck of Anya Mayor, the blonde woman who throws the sledgehammer. Part of IBM's fortune comes from machines sold to the Nazis during the Second World War. Perforated card machines allowed the maintenance of statistics. How many prisoners have been eliminated, Jews murdered? The rifle to the temple, gas into the neck, a naked body in the middle of a cold concrete room, eyes closed so as not to see the others, their fathers, their brothers, who fall in front of them. The bodies sag. There will be a mass grave. The Liberation will come too late. Millions marked by the war, almost ashamed of having to continue to live. During the 1985 Super Bowl, Apple attempts a new marketing coup: businessmen, eyes blindfolded, follow each other and fall one by one from the top of a cliff. The ad is called "Lemmings", in reference to the rodents known for their collective suicides. George Orwell was a pupil of Aldous Huxley. *Who are we?* is the title of a lecture given by the author of *Brave New World* in 1955 at Tarzana College in the state of California.

Zeus kills his father Cronos. Goya paints Saturn devouring his child. Whatever happened to Ellen Feiss? A millionaire boss who wears jeans and talks to young people is really cool. Jacques Cartier docks, it's July 24,

1534. Rivages sees himself at the foot of Cap Diamant for *Un été mer et monde*, that was in Quebec City in 1984. He's on a four-masted ship, the *Kruzenstern*. He raises his head. Up in the sails, Brautigan and Jobs sway in unison and chant loudly:

> I like to think
>   (it has to be!)
> of a cybernetic ecology
> where we are free of our labors
> and joined back to nature,
> returned to our mammal
> brothers and sisters,
> and all watched over
> by machines of loving grace.

Rivages closes his eyes. The effect of the drug dissipates. He begins to gnash his teeth. He trembles a little. He's back home. He brought back a tab of acid under the noses of the customs officers from California. He wanted it to end in color, fireworks, explosions of copper, sulfur barium, and titanium. But he just wants to throw up, forget all that. He found a new job. He starts in three days in the marketing department of a large publicly traded company. It's a company that develops applications for the iPhone, mostly games. He's made peace with himself. He still has some good years before liver or prostate cancer, or both. Next summer, he's off with his wife and his ten-year-old son. They will travel across California.

113

ONCE UPON A TIME

It took him three lives to understand that success is a fiction. It took him three fates to learn that to make a success of one's life is a story, that to make a success of one's life you must be able to tell a good story. It took him three lives to learn to tell his own. First there is his life up to the Mac. Then there is NeXT and Pixar. Finally, there's his life with the "i": iMac, iPod, iPhone, iPad.

It took him three lives to understand that happiness is only a fiction, that to be happy you have to invent your life, and that the only way to invent it is to tell it. This is what Rivages understood thanks to Weissmuller, Brautigan and Jobs. The value of man is not in laughter, the value of man is not in making tools. The value of man is in telling stories.

Once upon a time…

ESPLANADE
Books

THE FICTION SERIES AT VÉHICULE PRESS

 Véhicule Press